THE
PROSECUTOR
A NOVEL

Thomas Chastain

WILLIAM MORROW AND COMPANY, INC.
NEW YORK

It is the policy of William Morrow and Company, Inc., and its imprints and affiliates, recognizing the importance of preserving what has been written, to print the books we publish on acid-free paper, and we exert our best efforts to that end.

Library of Congress Cataloging-in-Publication Data

Chastain, Thomas.
    The prosecutor / by Thomas Chastain.
        p.   cm.
    ISBN 0-688-10088-0
    I. Title.
    PS3553.H3416P76   1992
    813'.54—dc20   91-47683
                                          CIP

Printed in the United States of America

First Edition

1 2 3 4 5 6 7 8 9 10

BOOK DESIGN BY MARIA DEMAIO

To everyone who
has helped—you
know who you are

1

The living room was carpeted in deep-pile beige, the walls a stark white backdrop for what Cavenaugh guessed were original oil paintings, the furniture a collection of overstuffed white sofas, love seats, armchairs. Pieces of sculpture on pedestals were here and there around the room. Toward the rear of the living room was a spiral staircase to the floor above.

The bodies were there, on the staircase. The first body was sprawled faceup five steps from the bottom of the staircase. Next to the body was a .380 automatic equipped with a silencer.

The second body lay eight steps from the top of the staircase, facedown. A .38 revolver was lying on the second step from the top of the staircase.

Both bodies were male, both had been shot.

Richard Krager was the dead man lying near the top of the stairs. There was blood from the exit wound near his left shoulder on the back of his blue silk pajamas.

The other man, identity still unknown to the police, was

dressed in a black turtleneck shirt, blue chinos, and Reeboks. He had been shot in the stomach.

That much the detectives had learned from Richard Krager's wife and from observation. Any other inspection of the bodies had to wait until the medical examiner, who had just arrived, officially declared the two men dead.

The wife, Bettina Krager, had phoned 911 and reported the shootings at 1:58 A.M. It was now 3:15 A.M.

Three of the detectives who had responded to the call, Cavenaugh and Detectives Edward Hirsch and Roberto Cruz, were in the living room. Detective Grace Zimmer had gone to the second floor with Bettina Krager, who wanted to change her clothes.

Detective Cruz looked at Cavenaugh. "You got the same feelings I have, Lieutenant; it was maybe an inside job? I mean whoever that guy was, he had to know something about how to get into the building, and into here."

"I haven't given the subject any thought yet," Cavenaugh said.

Cavenaugh, who was in charge at the scene, got rid of the two detectives then, sending them downstairs to question the building doorman. The doorman had already told them he didn't know anything about the shootings, or about how the unknown dead man might have gotten into the building and into the Krager apartment. Cavenaugh figured the doorman had been goofing off somewhere or sleeping at one time or another in the hours earlier and wasn't likely to change his story.

Cavenaugh just wanted Hirsch and Cruz out of the way before anybody else who would be involved in the investigation came to the apartment. It didn't look good to have three detectives standing around doing nothing even though by the book they had to wait until the M.E. finished examining the bodies.

Frank Cavenaugh was fifty years old, a heavyset man

with broad shoulders and a thick neck. His brown hair was graying on the sides and he was losing hair on the top of his head while gaining weight around his belt line, neither of which particularly bothered him. He thought of such matters as part of the inevitable process of life, impossible to alter and so to be endured, along with aging, the weather, the common cold, bad dreams.

He was a bred-in-the-bone cop, preceded in the department by his father and grandfather and followed by his only child, his daughter, Corinne, a new recruit undergoing training at the Police Academy.

Tonight Cavenaugh was edgy. He didn't want any screwups on the handling of this case. He already knew enough to know this shooting was going to have a high profile all the way up and down the line. After he'd sized up the situation he'd taken the precaution of phoning headquarters to request that the district attorney personally be notified. He wanted someone from the D.A.'s office to be present when he took an official statement from Bettina Krager.

Cavenaugh didn't keep up with public figures in the news all that much but he'd recognized who the Kragers were as soon as he heard the names; Richard Krager had been prominent in what was to Cavenaugh the netherworld of Wall Street big-bucks finance and the couple were regularly featured in news accounts of black-tie charity events.

"Hello, Frank. What have we got here?" Anne Gilman asked, coming in through the foyer.

"Hey," Cavenaugh said, turning to watch her walk toward him.

Anne Gilman had that quality sometimes described as presence, the natural projection of herself into a larger dimension than the space she physically occupied. At the moment she looked younger than her true age of thirty-six. Her dark hair was hidden under a scarf, her face was scrubbed clean of makeup, and there was the softness of sleep she'd just awakened from still in her face. She was wearing tailored slacks, a blouse, and sandals, and had a lightweight sweater draped around her shoulders, the arms of it hanging loose.

Cavenaugh swung around toward the staircase. "It looks like a bungled B and E. The one shot at the top of the stairs is Richard Krager. You know who he is?"

Anne Gilman nodded. "I know."

"Yeah well," Cavenaugh said. He paused then and they watched Bettina Krager come down the staircase followed by Grace Zimmer, both of them skirting carefully around the two bodies.

Cavenaugh introduced Bettina Krager to Anne Gilman. "Mrs. Krager, this is District Attorney Gilman."

"Oh, of course," Bettina said, shaking hands with Anne. "I've seen your picture in the papers and interviews you've done on TV. The camera likes you, you know."

Anne thought the remark curious, then decided the poor woman was simply slightly unstrung by the events of the night. Anne inclined her head. "Mrs. Krager."

Detective Grace Zimmer, thirty-four years old, of medium height, redheaded, stood in the background through the proceedings. She had newly made the rank of detective and studied the pros carefully.

Bettina Krager was dressed in a Chinese mandarin robe, ankle-length, and sandals. Her ash-blonde hair was pulled back tight on either side of her head in the manner ballet dancers often chose to wear their hair. Looking at her, Anne recalled that Bettina had been a dancer with the New York City Ballet before she had married Richard Krager. Anne remembered, too, that Bettina was twenty-five years old, about half her husband's age, and neither had been married previously.

Cavenaugh said, "What we need now, Mrs. Krager, is for you to answer some questions for us."

"I understand."

"Were you and your husband home all evening?"

Bettina said that they'd gone out early, around six-thirty, to a reception at Lincoln Center. Afterward, they had had dinner at Tavern on the Green in Central Park and had returned home about eleven-fifteen. She spoke haltingly and was obviously upset and ill at ease.

Anne Gilman glanced around the apartment as she listened to Bettina's answers to Cavenaugh's questions. She recognized the original oil paintings hanging on the walls, Matisse, Braque, Picasso, Pollock, Lichtenstein. She approved of the paintings if not much else of the look of the place which she imagined more expressed the taste of a decorator than of the Kragers themselves.

Cavenaugh asked, "You didn't notice anything unusual when you came back to the apartment?"

Bettina shook her head.

"Please continue."

She said they had gone to bed about midnight. The bedroom was right at the top of the stairs. She was asleep when she awakened suddenly to find her husband calling her name softly. He had whispered to her that he'd heard a sound from downstairs and was going to investigate. He cautioned her to be quiet.

"He went out into the hall and I saw the hall light go on. Then, almost immediately, I heard a couple, several, shots—at least I felt sure they were gunshots."

She paused and shook her head.

"Yes, and then?" Cavenaugh prompted.

"I—I got out of bed. Quietly. Richard kept a gun in the drawer of the night table between our beds. I took out the gun and tiptoed into the hall. I saw Richard lying near the top of the stairs. He wasn't moving. I saw the blood on the back of his pajamas. Then I looked down. I saw this figure on the stairs, this man coming up the stairs. He had his head down. I aimed the gun at him and I fired. I kept firing until the gun was empty and he had gone down. Then I—then I went to the phone and called nine-one-one. That's—what happened."

Cavenaugh asked her about the help they employed at the apartment.

She told him they employed a maid, a cook, a house-keeper, and a driver. She gave him their names and addresses.

Cavenaugh said, "All right, Mrs. Krager. That's all I need to know for now. In the morning I'd like you to come to the precinct and sign a statement. I'll have a car sent for you. About ten A.M., is that satisfactory?"

She nodded.

"Meanwhile," he suggested, "do you have somewhere you'd rather be for the rest of the night? A friend you could stay with, perhaps? My men are going to need to be here for a good while longer."

Bettina shook her head. "I think I'd rather stay here. I'll go up to the bedroom, be out of the way."

"Fine," Cavenaugh said. "If that's what you want to do."

Cavenaugh walked Anne Gilman out of the apartment. As they stood at the elevator, he said, "Any thoughts?"

Anne had worked with Cavenaugh on homicide cases from time to time in past years. She trusted him to handle the case so they'd have what they needed when they went to court. "Not really," she said. "I know you'll shake it all down. Just keep Charley Stenten fully informed."

Charley Stenten was chief homicide investigator for the D.A.'s office. "Charley'll have a full report on all we know up to then on his desk in the morning," Cavenaugh said. "Get a good night's sleep, A.G., or what's left of the night."

2

Anne Gilman was up early that morning after she had been at the Krager apartment, despite the fact that her sleep had been interrupted. She always liked to have a couple of hours alone in the house before her car and driver picked her up for the trip to her office in lower Manhattan.

Her house was a three-story brownstone on East Seventy-sixth Street just off Fifth Avenue. She had lived there all her life except for the four years she'd spent at Harvard Law School where she'd received her degree. The year she had graduated she had passed her bar exam and had gone to work in Manhattan as an assistant D.A.

She was an only child, born late in her parents' lives, when her mother, Elizabeth, was forty, and her father, Benjamin, was fifty. Her father had been one of the leading trial lawyers in New York and, later, a judge in Superior Court.

Benjamin Gilman had always been something of a formidable figure as a trial lawyer and even more so after he became a judge. Tall and always erect in posture, with deep-set dark eyes behind gold-rimmed glasses, he unfailingly wore custom-tailored suits with a vest, summer and winter. Anne ever after thought of him as he was described by one of her girl friends from Harvard she had brought home for a weekend, "He looks like he sleeps in a three-piece suit."

Elizabeth Gilman was, on the other hand, always described as "a serene beauty." She had a lovely, oval-shaped face, long black hair she wore coiled around the top of her head, and the same gold-flecked eyes Anne inherited.

Anne had grown up attending private schools in Manhattan, and since she lived so close to them, her playgrounds had been Central Park and the Metropolitan Museum of Art.

When she'd decided she wanted to study law she had imagined that she would try for a job with a law firm when she graduated. She'd never considered then going into any law enforcement agency.

Arthur Hillyard was the one who suggested she join the D.A.'s office for a year or so for the experience. Hillyard had been her father's best friend, a man who was a power behind the political scene in New York State. When Anne was older she recognized that Arthur Hillyard was what was known, in more recent times, as a power broker, a man who operated much as the old political bosses once did, exchanging a favor for a favor. She knew that Arthur Hillyard had smoothed the way for a Superior Court judgeship for her father just as later he had helped her into a job with the D.A.'s office.

Anne's parents were now dead, her father for ten years, her mother for five, and although the three-story brownstone that had been the family home was larger than she needed living alone, she had never been able to bring herself to sell it and get a smaller place. The house and almost everything in it were a reminder, a link to her earlier life, and so much of it would be gone forever if she gave them up. Too, they were, she acknowledged to herself, a refuge for her from the changing world, the changing city.

This morning, as almost every morning, she made breakfast for herself and took in the morning *New York Times*. She read the paper and listened to the news on the radio while she had breakfast. There was no mention of the shooting at the Krager apartment in the *Times*—the shooting had taken place too late to make the morning edition. The first story in the radio news, however, was an account of the crime, but there were only the basic facts reported with a brief background about Richard and Bettina Krager. Finishing her breakfast, she left the dishes for the housekeeper, Mrs. Blair, who came every day and kept the house in order.

As was her habit, Anne took her time dressing. Her mother had always had an eye for fashion and Anne had learned from her as well as developing her own style. It was a summer day and she chose a dark blue linen suit with a high V neck, dark sheer stockings, and black patent leather pumps. She had never, and would never, concede her femininity in the way she dressed to the work she did.

By the time she was ready to leave, the car was waiting for her in front of the house. She picked up her beeper from a bedside table and stuck it into the pocket of her jacket.

The car was a Chrysler Imperial. The driver, Detective Matt Slater, who also served as her bodyguard, was standing next to it, smoking a cigarette which he flipped away as he opened the rear door for her. Slater was the perfect driver. Other than his greeting, "Good morning, D.A. Gilman," and her answer, they would not speak again during the drive, yet it was a comfortable silence. In size and impassive demeanor Slater reminded Anne of the guards at Buckingham Palace. She was impressed by the way he drove, his eyes moving from the rearview mirror to the road ahead to the sideview mirror and then back to the road again, always observing the cars and traffic ahead, behind, and beside him.

They drove up to Seventy-ninth Street and across to the FDR Drive, then went south. The drive to work, as often, gave Anne time for reflection. She had always considered herself lucky to have been born in Manhattan and liked having lived in the city almost all her life. Despite all the problems in Manhattan—crime, and especially crime resulting from drugs—the environment of the city stimulated, challenged her, and recently, she had been rewarded with the job of district attorney, and at a time when she'd never expected to have a chance, so soon, of becoming D.A.

In fact, four months earlier, she hadn't really wanted to attend the reception at Gracie Mansion, the mayor's residence, to which she'd been invited one evening. In the ten years she had worked as an assistant district attorney in Manhattan she had tried to avoid politicians and political functions whenever she could. When she'd received that invitation, she phoned to decline, using the excuse of work.

But then she had gotten a phone call from Arthur Hillyard. He had called to say that he knew Anne had been invited to the reception that evening and that as a favor he wanted her to accompany him to Gracie Mansion.

So of course she had to accept.

Hillyard had picked her up in his limousine and as they drove to East End Avenue, he patted her hand and said, "My dear, I know you don't quite approve of these political soirées but it wouldn't hurt you to cultivate some of the influential people in this town. You never know when they might be able to help you."

"Or," Anne suggested, "vice versa, when they might feel that I'll be able to help them? Isn't that the way it works? That's what you call politics, isn't it?"

Arthur Hillyard was seventy-three years old, tall, silver-haired, his face strong, the skin smooth and pink, his suits custom-made, his shoes shined to a gloss, his fingernails manicured.

He laughed and said, "My dear, you haven't quite comprehended it yet but all of life is politics, one way or the other. Politics makes the world go around, like it or not. Not everyone has an entrée into being a player in politics. You do."

"Then maybe it's not politics I don't like but the players."

Hillyard laughed again. "You can be a player and not like the other players. That's part of politics, too. Anyway, I'm glad you agreed to come with me tonight."

In front of Gracie Mansion the limousines were lined up, police were directing traffic, spectators were crowding behind the wooden sawhorses across the street, lights streamed out of the windows of the mansion, and behind it a yacht cruised northward on the East River. At the front door of the mansion Anne and Hillyard were stopped by a member of the mayor's security detail and handed a card that had the seal of New York City stamped at the top and read:

> Please be advised that security guidelines are now in effect at Gracie Mansion and that for your protection all handbags, briefcases, and other hand-held packages may be subject to inspection. We apologize for any inconvenience this may cause.

Anne didn't know why she should have been shocked that the threat of violence was acknowledged even there in the very home of the city's highest elected official, but she was.

She handed over her small beaded handbag to the security guard, who quickly handed it back, and then she paused in the front hallway and took a quick look at her reflection in the mirror of her compact. Satisfied that she looked stylish in her black cocktail dress with the scooped neck, she moved ahead of Arthur Hillyard into a room full of people.

Hillyard was steering her to first one person and then another, city council members, a newspaper publisher, a real estate developer, several movie and stage actors and actresses. In ten years in the district attorney's office Anne had prosecuted several prominent homicide cases—her special talent—and some of the people there knew who she was though many others didn't. She had two glasses of wine, shook hands with the mayor, Kenneth Wyland, one of those present who didn't know who she was, she was sure, and then Arthur Hillyard took her arm and led her out of the room and down the hall to the library.

"There's a particular person here tonight who wants to talk to you," Hillyard said. He opened the door to the library and motioned Anne inside.

She was unprepared to encounter the man sitting alone in the room in a leather armchair near the windows.

Hillyard said, "Governor, this is Anne Gilman. I believe you wanted to have a talk with her."

"I did indeed," New York State Governor Edmund Pauling said, standing. "Ms. Gilman, come sit."

He motioned to the chair next to his. Hillyard said, "If you'll excuse me," and left the room, closing the door quietly behind him.

Anne's first impression of the governor was that he looked less stern, less reserved in manner, than he did in photographs and on television. He was still an imposing figure, well over six feet in height and physically trim, as he had kept himself since his early years at the Naval Academy before he had served as commander on a battleship and, later, entered politics. And there was also a gentleness about him, a courtliness, as he bowed slightly when she sat down.

She knew he was in his mid-fifties, his hair dark brown, his blue eyes direct and penetrating.

"Well now," he said, "would it surprise you to learn that I know a great deal about you?"

Anne was surprised and puzzled as she answered, "Yes. Yes, frankly, it would surprise me."

Pauling nodded. "You haven't been exactly an unknown in the news, you know. I followed several of the cases you successfully prosecuted. The Airport Strangler, the Soho Stabber." He smiled. "The names the news media give to these cases."

Anne smiled too. "It's all in the alliteration. Give them a case gory enough and they'll come up with a name for it."

"I know more about your work in the D.A.'s office than just the cases you've prosecuted. Bill Raney mentioned you several times in discussions we had in the past."

William Raney had been district attorney for the ten years Anne had worked as an assistant D.A. A week earlier Raney had suffered a stroke and was on leave recuperating.

"Almost everything I know I learned from District Attorney Raney," Anne said. "I don't think anyone could have a better teacher."

"Bill's been a force in law enforcement in this city," Pauling said. "No doubt about it."

He paused for a moment before he said, "What I'm about to tell you now is confidential, at least for the next twelve hours or so before it's announced publicly. Bill Raney won't be returning to the job of district attorney. I was so advised this morning."

Anne let a hand drop to the arm of her chair. "I'm sorry. I'm so sorry."

"Yes." Pauling moved forward in his chair. "Which is why I wanted to talk to you alone tonight. Bill's term has eleven months to run before the next election. As you know, in the event that an elected district attorney dies or is incapacitated while in office, it is the governor who must pick the person to serve until the time of the next election. I would like to appoint you as district attorney for the remainder of Bill Raney's term. The first female district attorney of Manhattan."

Anne was taken by surprise. She started to say something, then stopped and leaned back in her chair.

Pauling said, "I would like to release the story of Bill's retirement tomorrow morning and then announce your appointment in the afternoon. Well, what's your answer?"

"I'm speechless," Anne managed to say. "Almost literally."

Pauling laughed. "If you're offering that as one of your qualifications for the job, I don't think it's a very high recommendation. What's wrong? Does taking on the job scare you?"

Anne had regained her composure. "Not at all," she said firmly. "It's just that I didn't think I'd have the job this soon."

Pauling looked at her keenly. "I assume then that you have given some thought from time to time of becoming D.A. one day?"

Anne's answer was direct. "Yes. I know it's a tough job. But one I can handle."

"Good then. We'll consider it settled." He started to rise from his chair.

"One question," Anne said quickly.

"Yes?"

She was frowning. "What happens at the end of eleven months? When election time comes up?"

"That depends," Pauling said, "upon how things go in the D.A.'s office for the next eleven months and upon whether or not you'd want to run for office."

"And if I got the party's nomination, wouldn't that be a factor?" Anne asked.

The governor nodded. "That, too." He stood. "Now, shall we consider the appointment settled?"

Anne said, "Yes."

The following day the governor announced her appointment as district attorney.

3

Charley Stenten didn't know why it should surprise him so much whenever he saw a truly beautiful woman who looked sad, but it always did. He supposed it was because he thought a beautiful woman started out in life with such an automatic advantage there should be little that could make her sad. Of course, in reality, he knew that such a thought was ridiculous. After all, the woman he was observing now who had prompted his thought had plenty to look sad about; even women as beautiful as Bettina Krager would hardly be untouched by the death, the murder, of a husband a few hours earlier.

Stenten was sitting on a ledge of the fountain in front of the Plaza Hotel on Fifth Avenue. Bettina Krager sat on a bench a dozen feet away, her back to him.

The report of the shooting of Richard Krager had been on Stenten's desk when he'd arrived at work in the D.A.'s office this morning. The report had stamped on it in red ink: TOP PRIORITY. Stenten had read the report quickly. There was a note attached from Lieutenant Cavenaugh saying that

Bettina Krager would be at the 16th Precinct between 10:00 A.M. and 11:00 A.M. to sign a statement.

Stenten had gone there in time to see her, staying out of her sight, so he could tail her after she left the precinct. Nowhere in the records of the shooting of Richard Krager was there any suggestion that his wife was a suspect in the crime. There was no need for the suggestion; the unwritten rule in an as-yet-unsolved homicide was that the spouse was always considered a prime suspect, until eliminated by investigation.

Stenten believed it was important to put a suspect under surveillance as soon as possible when there was a homicide. After Bettina had signed her statement and a police car had driven her back to her apartment, Stenten had followed.

When she had gone inside the building Stenten had waited across the street on a bench near the wall running the length of Central Park along Fifth Avenue. He had a copy of *The New York Times* that provided him with a cover from behind which he could observe the entrance to Bettina's apartment building and the street around him.

The day was sunny, the sky clear, and there near the Sixty-sixth Street entrance to Central Park was a constant motion of traffic and pedestrians along the streets and sidewalks and into and out of the park. Buses, cars, and vans moved southward constantly one after another, and people streamed by, nurses or mothers pushing baby carriages, joggers, mostly female, some people, both men and women, well-dressed, others in shorts and T-shirts, and yet others carelessly dressed as if they had never bothered to glance at the mismatched clothing they wore. And others, inevitable nowadays, the displaced persons—as Stenten thought of them—more often called the homeless. Stenten had sometimes speculated that if most true New Yorkers had ambivalent love-hate feelings about Manhattan it was because the city itself was constantly changing, as now on this street, in the perception of those who inhabited it.

Charley Stenten knew himself to be a true New Yorker. Most cops working in the city were, had to be, true New Yorkers. He didn't believe cops were in any way special people and, yes, there were good cops and bad cops. But he did believe that to be a good cop you had to be a true New Yorker.

Stenten, who was thirty-nine years old, was dark-haired, slim, of medium height. He had been born in and grew up in Paramus, New Jersey. He had come to Manhattan after he graduated from high school and found work as a clerk in a small law office on lower Broadway. While he worked there he started taking courses at John Jay College of Criminal Justice. In time he earned a B.A. and, what was equally important, had made friends with several police officers who also were attending the college. That was when he decided to become a cop.

He had worked with a partner in a squad car, had been promoted to sergeant, was assigned to homicide, and had been lucky enough to be in on the investigation of two of the city's biggest cases, the Airport Strangler and the Soho Stabber. On both cases he had worked with then-assistant D.A. Anne Gilman and had been promoted again, to lieutenant. When Anne Gilman became district attorney she had offered him the position of chief homicide investigator for the D.A.'s office and he had accepted.

After an hour of watching the apartment building across the street, Stenten spotted Bettina Krager coming out and starting to walk south on Fifth Avenue. She had changed clothes and was wearing a blue denim halter dress, sandals, oversized sunglasses with dark blue lenses, and a Yankees baseball cap. Nobody who passed her on the street would recognize her from the photographs in the newspapers that always showed her in high-fashion evening gowns.

Stenten followed her, from the opposite side of the street, down Fifth Avenue to Central Park South and the square in front of the Plaza Hotel, where she finally stopped and sat on one of the stone benches. Stenten circled around the fountain in the center of the square and sat on one of the ledges where he could keep her in view.

As far as he could tell she could be just out for a stroll. Or she could be waiting to meet someone.

Time passed.

Stenten watched her, watched the people passing on the sidewalk near her. He noticed a man, a young man, cross Central Park South and walk past Bettina. The man didn't look directly at her as he passed and went on to the corner of Fifty-eighth Street, stopped and turned back. Stenten was watching the man carefully now, was watching Bettina too. Stenten saw her look directly at the man then look away. The man stopped and sat down on the bench next to her and Stenten saw that she appeared startled when the man spoke to her. Maybe the guy was just trying to pick her up, Stenten thought, but he didn't quite believe it.

And then he knew it wasn't just an attempted pickup when he saw that the two of them were talking back and forth and suddenly Bettina was standing and the man too was standing. When she started to walk away, the man grabbed her arm and spoke again but she freed her arm, turned, and walked quickly away back up Fifth Avenue.

The man stood watching her. Stenten sat watching him.

The man was in his twenties, Stenten guessed, about five six, underweight, his blond hair long and in a ponytail. A guy who wore his hair in a ponytail was, in Stenten's book, a horse's ass, never mind the rest of the way he looked. In the case of this guy, the rest of the way he looked wasn't all that great either. He was dressed in a short-sleeved shirt, the buttons open to midchest to show off the gold chains draped around his neck, dirty jeans, frayed espadrilles, no socks.

The man walked across Fifth Avenue and on to Lexington Avenue. Stenten followed him to the Lexington Avenue subway, on the subway down to Astor Place, and for two blocks after they got off the subway to a small apartment building on East Ninth Street. The man used a key to open the street door to the building and disappeared inside.

Stenten made notes of what he'd observed and headed back to his office, wondering what the connection could be between Bettina Krager and the guy who appeared to be such a lowlife.

4

The small white paneled van was parked on the crest of a rise of ground at the far edge of the Bethany Cemetery in Queens. Lieutenant John Holland of the NYPD Organized Crime Task Force was in the back of the van. Holland headed up the team of five detectives who were also in the back of the van, Grisham, Jankowitz, Martino, Myler, and Callie Brinnin.

Holland was looking out of the one-way window that on the outside was indistinguishable from the rest of the paneling on the side of the surveillance van. Twin video cameras were mounted at the window, each camera equipped with high-powered zoom lenses capable of focusing close up on objects as far away as the entrance to the cemetery.

The sun, midpoint in the sky, radiated heat through the roof of the van. From the high point of ground the skyline of Manhattan to the west could be seen shimmering in the gaseous haze of the day.

Callie Brinnin wiped the sweat from her pretty black-skinned face with a handkerchief and said, "A steam bath like this, man, ought to melt some pounds off me. I wonder if any of those diet freaks ever thought of trying this as a way to lose weight."

"Maybe we can patent the method," Martino said. "Buy us an old van, rent a patch of ground in the cemetery, and sell memberships. Call it the Fat Fryers Club, you get it? Fat F-r-y-e-r-s Club." Which elicited boos and groans from the rest of the team.

Holland, watching out of the window, had a pair of binoculars slung by a strap around his neck. He flicked some of the sweat from his face with his hand. His face was well-defined by forty-three years of a life of a considerable amount of determination that had etched lines around the corners of his mouth and dark brown eyes. His hair was black and cut short to police regulations. In size, he had never had any problem keeping his weight in proportion with his height of two inches under six feet.

He saw a hearse coming through the gates of the cemetery. "Heads up, guys," he said. "Here they come, I think."

Grisham and Myler moved into position to man the two video cameras; Jankowitz, Martino, and Callie Brinnin came over near Holland behind Grisham and Myler and the video cameras. Holland, with the binoculars, was tracking the hearse and the cortege of black limousines behind it as they drove slowly into the cemetery.

"Got 'em in view," Grisham said, at one of the video cameras. "I'm filming."

"Same here," Myler said.

Holland followed the line of vehicles as they came closer and finally stopped in the center of the cemetery near an open grave with chairs arranged around it and a canopy on four poles over it.

"They're right in focus," Myler said. "I can even read the name stamped into the brass plate on the side of the hearse, Furelli Funeral Home."

"Watch it!" Holland said. "They're starting to get out of the cars."

28

It was ironic, Holland thought, for almost a quarter of a century now the police department had been trying to nail Terrence McCord, the guy who was about to be buried. McCord had run the biggest burglary ring in New York City for decades and had never served a single day in jail. A couple of nights ago McCord had died in bed in his sleep of a heart attack. This guy who, in the course of a lifetime, had stolen millions, who had been the target of the best anticrime squads in the NYPD, not to mention who had managed to coexist with the five organized crime families in the tristate area, goes to sleep one night and dies peacefully at age eighty-one. The guy had led a charmed criminal life, was the only way you could figure it.

Starting almost three decades ago, Terry McCord had put together a gang primarily of Irishmen who burglarized the Seventh Avenue garment district, hijacked trucks, stole shipments intended for the city's department stores, made off with cargo coming into local airports. Sometimes the police were successful in making arrests in the robberies and convicting the ones they'd caught in the act but they had never been able to get enough evidence against McCord himself to put him away. None of the members of the burglary ring who were caught would, or could, implicate Terrence McCord.

What was equally charmed about McCord's criminal career was that the five organized crime families who controlled practically all of the vice in Manhattan—drugs, prostitution, illegal gambling, extortion, and most of the large-scale burglaries that were not the work of McCord's ring—allowed him to operate—although not without demanding a payoff from every job he masterminded. For years there had been this uneasy alliance between the organized crime families and the Irish gang.

One of the reasons John Holland and the members of his task force were at the cemetery to videotape the proceedings at the funeral was to record exactly who of the organized crime families showed up.

Another reason was to find out, if possible, who might be succeeding McCord in running the burglary ring.

Holland had his binoculars focused on the first limousine behind the hearse as the car door opened. He didn't recognize the man who stepped out, but he said, "Get a good shot of that guy."

Through the binoculars Holland could see the man lean back inside the car and offer his hand to a woman who next stepped out. Holland couldn't see the face of the woman since she was wearing a black veil. A couple of other men climbed out of the car and the woman walked between them toward the open grave as the man who had first emerged from the limousine turned toward those who were approaching him from the other cars lined up in the cemetery.

Holland recognized several of those men: Joey Rocco, Nick "Mule" Manko, Albert Marteen, all members of organized crime families, as they shook hands with the man standing next to the first limousine. Then others joined them in a circle around the man. Whoever the man was, Holland assumed he was the one who would be taking over the burglary operation.

As the casket was removed from the hearse and the group followed behind it to the grave, Grisham, who was bent over one of the video cameras, said, "I'm filming a real rogues' gallery here."

Holland nodded. His attention was centered on the scene at the grave site. There, even as the world was at last rid of old Terry McCord, stood a man ready to replace him—and the burglaries, robberies, and hijackings would go on. Of course Holland knew, as a cop, it was the way of the world in which he worked. The sons of bitches died, or you killed them, or you put them in prison, and there was always another son of a bitch to fill the vacuum nature abhors in all matters.

5

Anne Gilman sometimes thought that in the time since she'd taken over the job of D.A. a record of all the discovered criminal depravity in the city had crossed her desk in the form of indictments for trial. Murder, rape, sodomy, assault, extortion, fraud, robbery, and drugs, among other indictable criminal offenses. She finished reviewing the last of the papers of indictment that had reached her that day. Most of the decisions she had to make were to approve or question those cases involving recommendations from the various assistant D.A.s to plea-bargain the charges.

In the late afternoon the sky outside her office in the Frank Hogan Building had turned black and through the window she could see zagged flashes of lightning and hear the distant muted sound of thunder. There was a tap on her office door and Jenny Corso came in carrying a small tray.

"Coffee break, boss," Jenny said, placing the tray on Anne's desk.

Anne, as D.A., had a team of four secretaries working for her. Jenny Corso had been the executive secretary for the last four years William Raney was in office and Anne had arranged to have her promoted to administrative assistant, which didn't change her duties but improved her title. Jenny had an M.A. from Columbia University in political science. She was a cheerful, savvy twenty-nine-year-old lucky enough to have been born with brains, unlucky enough to have an aged mother and aunt to support in Howard Beach in Queens who took up most of her time when she wasn't working. Anne thought her brighter than some of the assistant D.A.s and had encouraged her to get her degree in law, but Jenny liked what she was doing and was content to remain in her present job.

Anne took a sip of coffee and said, "Thanks, Jenny. You spoil me."

"It's okay. You never ask me to do it, so I don't mind."

"Well, thanks anyway." Anne handed Jenny the papers she had finished reviewing. "Send these on their way and then why don't you take off. Maybe you can beat the storm."

The intercom on Anne's desk buzzed. Anne leaned forward and pressed the intercom key. "Yes?"

One of the secretaries in the outer office said, "Charley Stenten's here. He wants to know if you can see him."

"Send him in."

"See you, boss," Jenny said, going out as Charley Stenten came into the office, and closing the door behind her.

"You look beat, Charley," Anne said. "Sit down. What's up?"

Stenten had pulled his necktie loose and opened his shirt collar. He still had on a cord jacket, crisply pressed from the dry cleaners that morning, now wrinkled from the heat of the day. He told her about his surveillance of Bettina Krager earlier in the day and about the man Bettina had encountered in front of the Plaza Hotel.

Anne was frowning. "You think she went there to meet him?"

"It sure looked that way," Stenten said. "On the other hand, from the time she left her apartment building she didn't give any indication that she cared whether she was being followed, watched, or not. She never looked around her and behind her even once."

"It could be that it never occurred to her that she'd be under surveillance."

"There's that, yeah." Stenten nodded. "Or maybe she didn't think she had anything to hide. Anyhow, this afternoon I talked it over with Frank Cavenaugh. He's going to assign a man to check on this guy with the ponytail, see if we can get a line on him. Meanwhile, Cavenaugh told me they haven't gotten an ID on the intruder who was shot in the Krager apartment. They're working on it. I get the feeling Cavenaugh wants this case wrapped up fast and out of the way, out of the news. He says that order came direct from the commissioner."

Anne looked at Stenten carefully. "Meaning what, Charley?"

"Meaning, I'd venture to say, the cops would be just as happy if they made the whole thing into a simple break-in where Krager got shot and Bettina Krager killed the burglar the way she said she did. Homicide solved, the whole thing goes away."

"I don't know, Charley," Anne said. "Frank Cavenaugh's too straight to let that happen. I think."

Stenten waved a hand in the air. "Hey, don't get me wrong about Frank. If he has his way the case won't get shut down too soon. The trouble is that decision might be taken away from him somewhere along the way."

Anne leaned forward at the desk. "Tell me what makes you think it wasn't just a double homicide growing out of a simple burglary in progress?"

Stenten waved his hand in the air again. "Hey! Hey! Hey! I didn't say I thought it was anything else. I just want to be sure it wasn't anything else. And that means a thorough investigation of everybody and everything connected with Richard Krager's homicide."

Anne smiled. "You're my boy, Charley. We're both wondering about the same thing, aren't we? I've been wondering about it ever since I left that apartment last night. Her."

"Her," Stenten agreed. "What could have happened fits all the known facts as easily as what she says happened. What could have happened is she hires a guy to kill her husband. She arranges it so the guy can get into her apartment after she and the husband go to bed. She listens until she hears the killer enter the apartment, she rouses her husband, he goes to investigate and—bang—the killer shoots him dead. And before the killer can get out of the apartment she's there with her husband's gun and—another bang—and the hired killer's dead. She's free and clear and look at all that money I would guess she's going to inherit. I'm not positive it happened that way but—"

Anne's phone rang, interrupting Stenten.

Anne said, "Hold it a minute," and answered the phone.

Assistant D.A. Rebecca Cohen on the other end of the line said, "A.G., the court just notified me the jury's about to return with a verdict on Lewis Bevvers. I'd really, really, really like it if you'd be there with me when they come in. I'm leaving now."

"I'll be there," Anne said, disconnected the line, and called Detective Steve Alison at headquarters. He answered on the first ring and Anne said quickly, "This is D.A. Gilman, the jury's on its way in with a verdict on Lewis Bevvers. Are you all set?"

"All set," Alison said. "I'll see you in court."

Anne hung up the phone. She stood and went to the closet behind her desk to get an umbrella as she said to Stenten, "The jury's returning with a verdict in the Bevvers case." She looked back over her shoulder. "Finish what you were saying about the Krager shooting."

34

Stenten was standing. "I was saying I'm not positive it happened the way I was theorizing but I'd sure like to see a thorough investigation conducted."

"So would I," Anne said firmly. "And I'll tell you this: If you aren't satisfied at the way the commissioner or anybody else handles the investigation, we'll run our own. I want you to stay on the case. That's an order."

Stenten grinned. He said softly, "You're my girl, Anne."

6

Anne came into the court-
room quickly and walked forward to a seat at the prosecution
table as Judge Orrin Burroughs took his place on the bench
in Room 521 of the Criminal Courts Building at 100 Centre
Street. The bailiff called the court to order and there was a
stillness in the room in the interval before the jury appeared.

Anne smiled reassuringly at Assistant D.A. Rebecca Cohen who sat in the chair next to her. Anne could see that
under the table Rebecca had her legs crossed and her left
foot was swinging back and forth.

The two women were the same age. The assistant D.A.
was a slim, intense woman. Her complexion was pale and her
brown hair which fell to her shoulders was slightly dishev-
eled. She sat forward on her chair, slump-shouldered. Anne
knew how hard Rebecca had worked on the prosecution of
the case against the defendant, Lewis Bevvers, and how much
it would mean to Rebecca if the jury brought in a guilty
verdict against him.

To the right of where Anne and Rebecca sat was the
defense table, where Lewis Bevvers and his lawyer, Martin

Groger, sat. Anne let her eyes rest for a moment on Lewis Bevvers. He was sitting straight in his chair, his right hand resting on top of his left hand on the table in front of him. Upright, his attitude was signaling. He was a man of medium height, his black hair parted neatly on the left side. He had an angular face with a black mustache not much larger than a line drawn across his upper lip with a felt-tip pen would be. He was fifty years old but could have, and probably had, passed himself off as five to ten years younger.

Nothing about him looked particularly out of the ordinary, Anne thought, and certainly nothing you could detect from his appearance would make you suspect he had preyed upon and murdered God-only-knew-how-many women for their savings.

In court today he was going to be sentenced or not for only a single murder, the murder of one Lucille Etherton, whose body—like the bodies of the other women he was suspected of murdering—had never been found.

The prosecution's case, presented during the trial, had been based on circumstantial evidence. Testimony that he had lived with Lucille Etherton for six months, that she had disappeared without a trace, that he subsequently had disposed of her house and possessions, that just prior to her death she had withdrawn her life savings of fifty thousand dollars from the bank. Finally, there had been what the prosecution believed would be its strongest evidence. In the basement of the brownstone on West Ninety-seventh Street where Bevvers had moved and to which the police had traced him were found bloodstains that DNA testing concluded were Lucille Etherton's bloodstains.

All in the D.A.'s office—including Anne—believed they didn't have as strong a case against Bevvers as they'd liked to have had. But they had also agreed that if Bevvers were guilty, as they suspected, of a string of murders—several of which the police were still investigating—they should try to get him off the streets before he claimed any more victims.

Anne had attended many of the court sessions during the trial. She believed Rebecca Cohen had done a good job in arguing the prosecution's charges. If the jury brought in a verdict of not guilty it would be, Anne believed, because Bevvers's lawyer had pulled off another of the courtroom tricks that had made him famous or infamous, according to his admirers or detractors.

Anne was one of the latter and not only for what she regarded as his shoddy courtroom tactics. There was about him in appearance as well as actions the deliberate flaunting of an insufferable arrogance and ego.

Sitting half turned in his seat, Groger had one arm draped over the back of the chair as if to show himself off to the spectators. A big man, broad in the chest, he had a thick mane of white hair, a ruddy complexion, bushy black eyebrows, thick lips, and a mouthful of teeth that had either been capped or were false.

The pulling-the-rabbit-out-of-the-hat trick Groger had employed during the Lewis Bevvers trial was to produce a last-minute surprise witness. The witness, Martha Turner, testified that during the last six-month period when the missing Lucille Etherton was seen and then disappeared Bevvers and Martha Turner had been living together. She further testified that in that time the other woman frequently phoned Bevvers, pleading with him to return to her. It was Martha Turner's testimony that Lucille Etherton had even given Bevvers many of her personal possessions and the deed to her house in an attempt to get him back. Finally, according to the witness, Lucille Etherton had phoned Bevvers at the house where he was living with Martha Turner to announce that she had sadly realized he was never coming back and was withdrawing her savings and moving out west.

Martha Turner was a plain-looking, middle-aged woman who had never married and Anne didn't believe her to be a very credible witness. In fact, there were a dozen or so similar-looking women who attended every day of the trial openly in support of Bevvers. Anne could only conclude that all of these women were typical of the victims Lewis Bevvers managed to attract to himself. Still, she knew that the testimony of Martha Turner, credible or not, would have influence on any jury in a case where all the evidence was circumstantial.

There was a stir as a door to the courtroom opened and the jury filed in.

Anne leaned close to Rebecca Cohen and whispered, "Whatever happens now, I want you to know, speaking for all of us in the D.A.'s office, you did a terrific job. We're all proud of you."

Judge Burroughs's clerk addressed the seated jurors. "Will the foreman please rise."

The foreman, an MTA bus driver, got to his feet quickly.

"Has the jury agreed upon a verdict?" the clerk asked.

"We have," the foreman said slowly. "We find the defendant, on the charge of murder in the second degree, not guilty."

There was a confusion of sounds from the spectators, some approving, some disapproving the verdict, the judge calling for order, then dismissing Lewis Bevvers, and thanking the jurors.

Rebecca sat shaking her head.

A crowd of women spectators was surrounding Bevvers at the defense table; Martin Groger had his arms raised in a victory symbol.

Anne turned and looked at Detective Steve Alison who had come forward from the back of the courtroom. She nodded to him. She watched as he crossed to Bevvers and Groger, took some papers from his inside jacket pocket, showed the papers to the two men, grabbed Bevvers by the arm, and propelled him through the spectators toward the entrance to the courtroom.

Martin Groger trailed after the two men briefly, gesturing furiously, sputtering words Anne couldn't hear, before finally coming to a stop. He then spun around quickly and came charging toward the defense table, a finger jabbing the air in the direction of Anne.

Groger advanced so close up to Anne that for a moment she thought he was going to keep coming and bowl her over. "What," he demanded, his flushed face only inches from hers, "in the hell do you think you're doing, Ms.—" he repeated, "Ms.—District Attorney of Manhattan?"

"You saw the papers of indictment," Anne said, her voice steady. "I have ordered the arrest of your client, Lewis Bevvers, on a finding by the grand jury charging him with the murder of one Shirley Thomasson in January of last year."

Groger said loudly, "By God, you won't get away with this. It's nothing less than deliberate harassment of my client!"

"Tell it to a judge," Anne said, motioning to Rebecca to leave with her, then turning back to say, "Incidentally, this time the prosecution's asking for a million dollars in bail. See you in court, Groger."

Anne and Rebecca left the courtroom.

In the elevator Rebecca let out a small squeal of delight. "You really sandbagged that son of a bitch. It was delicious!"

"Yes." Anne nodded in agreement, hoping to banish a slight feeling of claustrophobia. "But I want you to get together with Steve Alison right away. They'll be interrogating Bevvers about Shirley Thomasson. Then he'll be arraigned. I think we can get a million dollars' bail set which ought to keep him locked up until we go to trial. Another thing, Rebecca, when he goes back on trial I want you to handle the prosecution again."

"Thanks, thanks," Rebecca said, obviously pleased. "I'd like nothing better than to get another shot at him."

Anne smiled. "Well, you're going to get it."

When the elevator reached the first floor Anne could see that the steps outside the courthouse were filled with TV

cameras, reporters, and photographers waiting to get a statement from the prosecution and the defense in the Bevvers
trial.

Anne's beeper signal began to sound. She took the
beeper from her pocket and glanced at the digital numbers
of the caller trying to reach her.

She said, "You go ahead, Rebecca, talk to the reporters.
Let me take care of this call."

Anne veered away from the entrance to the courthouse
and went down the lobby to the rear of the building where
there was a row of public telephones. She dialed the number
showing on her signal beeper.

"Yes, help you?" the voice on the other end of the line
asked.

She said, "Hi."

"Hello there."

"I'll be ready at eight P.M. Okay?"

"Okay. Fine."

She disconnected the line and went back through the
lobby. At the door she could see Rebecca being interviewed
by reporters halfway down the steps and Martin Groger being interviewed at the top of the steps. Anne lowered her
head, raised her umbrella to shield her face, and managed to
get down the steps without being noticed by the newsmen.
She wanted to stay out of the picture; the moment belonged
to Rebecca Cohen.

The district attorney's office was just around the corner
from the Criminal Courts Building. She hurried because the
rain had begun to fall and because she wanted to finish her
work for the day and get home early.

7

Charley Stenten sat at the bar in Dresner's Restaurant at Seventy-eighth Street and York Avenue drinking a Budweiser draft and watching the rain stream down the glass front of the restaurant facing York Avenue. He had come there directly from the office on the subway. He lived only a block away, at the Pavilion on Seventy-seventh Street between York and the East River. Stenten was a regular at the bar. He had become good friends with most of the regulars who hung out there including several retired NYPD detectives who lived in the neighborhood. Probably because of the weather none of the others were there, although the bar was practically filled, as usual, and there were already early customers at the tables and booths in the restaurant area beyond the partition that separated the dining room and the bar.

He had had two Bud drafts and was about to leave when Frank Cavenaugh came in through the door, taking off his rain-soaked hat and raincoat and hanging them on the clothes hooks near the front of the bar. Stenten was surprised to see him there since Cavenaugh lived on the west side of Manhattan.

Cavenaugh pulled up a barstool next to Stenten and said, "I was hoping I'd catch you here. I tried to reach you at the office but you'd just left."

"Yeah? What's up, Frank?"

Cavenaugh ordered a shot of whiskey and a draft beer and said, "We got an ID on the dead guy in the Krager case. I thought you'd want to know."

"Sure," Stenten said. "Tell me." He did think it was curious that Cavenaugh would believe the news was urgent enough to make an out-of-the-way stop at the bar so Stenten would know.

"The guy's name was Kenneth Shuba. He ran one of those video rental shops down on Second Avenue." Cavenaugh drank the shot of whiskey. "When they were going through his clothes after the body got to the morgue one of the forensic people found a card in his pants pocket that had the name and address of the video shop on it. Funny thing is there was nothing else in any of his pockets. The card was all bent out of shape and stuffed way down in his pocket. Like maybe somebody searched him but missed finding the card."

Cavenaugh took a sip of beer and said, "Anyhow, since that was all we had to go on, we checked out the video shop. There was a girl working there. She said her boss, Shuba, hadn't come in today. We described the guy we had at the morgue. She said, yeah, it sounded like Shuba. We took her to the morgue. She positively identified the body."

"I don't guess there's been time yet to check whether or not he's got a record?" Stenten asked.

Cavenaugh ran a hand through his thinning hair. "At headquarters they're running a search through Washington's National Crime Information Center to see if anything shows up. There's something more, though, and this you're going to love!"

Stenten knew he was about to find out what had brought Cavenaugh to the bar to seek him out. He said, "Let's hear it."

Cavenaugh grinned. "The girl who worked for Shuba told us where he lived. The same building we've had under surveillance today since you told us it was where the other guy lived. The guy with the ponytail who met Bettina Krager in front of the Plaza Hotel."

Stenten swallowed hard. "Both guys lived in the same building?"

Cavenaugh nodded. "Looks like you hit some kind of pay dirt. Some kind of connection between Shuba, Bettina Krager, and a guy who lives in the same building as Shuba did. If there's no connection it'd have to be a hell of a coincidence. Since it's thanks to you that we know at least this much, does it make you happy?"

"Hell, I don't know," Stenten said slowly, surprising himself.

"What do you mean, you don't know? Up until you told us about the meeting she and the guy had the case was all but written off as a burglary homicide."

Stenten shook his head. "I know. I know."

"So?"

Stenten shook his head again. "So, yeah, I guess I'm glad." He thought for a moment. Then he said, "Now, what I guess I'm worried about is that with the little bit we know we'll go too fast the other way."

Cavenaugh said, "You know what your problem is, Charley? Before, you didn't like the way we were figuring the case because it seemed too neat and simple to you. That's the kind of mind you have. I know that's what it is with you. So, let me just remind you that if Bettina Krager is somehow involved in the murder of her husband there's going to be no way too neat and simple to prove it. Does that make you feel better?"

Stenten nodded. But he wasn't sure he did feel better.

Cavenaugh finished his beer and shoved himself up from the barstool.

Stenten said, "Look, Frank. Thanks for telling me. I'll pass the information on to the boss. I know she'd like to get this one wrapped up as quickly as possible."

Cavenaugh had his hat and coat on.

"Be talking to you, Charley," he said.

"Thanks again, Frank."

Stenten watched Cavenaugh, head lowered, hurry out into the pouring rain. He then ordered another beer and drank it slowly, wondering why in the hell he was—what? Depressed about the news Cavenaugh had brought him? He was depressed and the reason was—and he hadn't realized it until this moment—he was attracted to Bettina Krager. He didn't want to believe she could be connected to the murder of her husband.

The sudden realization that he felt that way about her troubled him. Here she was all but a prime suspect in a homicide case he was investigating. This was a new, and dangerous, experience for him. He'd have to watch his step. And his emotions.

Anne Gilman stood at the window in her living room, watching the rain falling in sheets that gushed up and down and back and forth with the changing direction of the wind along the block of East Seventy-sixth Street.

She had arrived home an hour earlier, had fixed herself a martini, and had had a steaming hot shower. Afterward, she had painted her fingernails and toenails, put on lipstick and eye shadow, and brushed her hair. She went to the closet and took out a sheer pale pink negligee. She put it on and stepped into a pair of gold sandals. When she had come downstairs it was a few minutes before eight.

Standing at the window she saw a car turn into the driveway next to her house. The driveway led to a two-car garage connected to the house. There was a door leading directly into the house and after a couple of minutes she heard a key in the lock of the door. The door opened.

"Hey!" she said. "Did you get wet?"

"Not a drop. I'm dry from door to door. You know what? You look terrific. Very sexy."

She laughed. "That was the idea." She spread her arms, knowing she was back-lighted provocatively from a lamp in the living room behind her. "If I look that sexy, why are we standing here wasting time?"

"I thought you would never ask."

"Hurry, hurry, hurry," she said softly, and then, "Um, um, um, that's nice. Yes, it feels so good."

"You keep that up and we'll never make it upstairs. But don't stop."

"Ah, oh!" she whispered. "We do fit well together, don't we?"

There was no more talking for the rest of the way upstairs, only soft murmurs from her.

8

Wednesday morning, two days after Lieutenant John Holland and his Organized Crime Task Force had videotaped Terrence McCord's funeral, Holland met with Anne Gilman in her office. Two members of his team were also present, Callie Brinnin and Fred Myler. Anne had called Assistant D.A. Will Cowper to sit in on the meeting.

Cowper had worked in the D.A.'s office for ten years. He was a gangly man, in his late thirties, with sandy hair. His eyeglasses were blue-tinted and he always wore a polka-dot bow tie. Today the polka dots matched the color of his tinted glasses.

Holland briefly explained what they were about to see and inserted the videotape into the office VCR.

"This is a premiere film," Holland said. "The debut of the newest big gun on the organized crime scene."

He pressed the play button and kept up a running commentary as the videotape ran. "Notice the guy getting out of the first car. We're almost sure he's the one taking over the McCord gang. We don't know much about him yet. The

Intelligence Unit is trying to develop information on him. We know his name is Roy Clayton."

Holland pressed the freeze-frame button on the VCR and the face of Roy Clayton remained in close-up on the TV screen. He had swarthy skin, black hair, thick black eyebrows, dark eyes. Holland judged him to be thirtysomething.

While the face remained, like a "Wanted" poster, on the TV screen, Holland said, "There's one other thing we know about him. For years old Terrence McCord owned a club up in Harlem, called it Easy Street, which he used as his head-quarters. We bugged the place from time to time but never picked up anything we could use. Anyhow, according to the Intelligence Unit, about six months ago this guy, Clayton, first showed up at McCord's club and was always around. Nobody could ever figure out if he was a bouncer or manager or what. But he was there most of the time."

"You sure this is the guy who's going to take over Mc-Cord's operation?" Will Cowper asked.

"Take a look at this," Holland said, and pressed the play button. On-screen appeared the men who had been video-taped at the cemetery getting out of their limousines and greeting Roy Clayton.

Holland identified them. "Joey Rocco, *consigliere,* coun-selor, second-in-command, of the Boglio family. Nick "Mule" Manko, *capo regima,* captain, of the Terrizi family. Al Mar-teen, under boss of the Rigletto family. Joseph Joseph "Joe-Joe" Carnerie, don, boss of bosses, of the Franshetti family. Representatives of four out of the five organized crime fam-ilies in New York–New Jersey. We're working on the IDs of some of the others we photographed but didn't recognize. Notice how when they all pay their respects to Clayton they practically kiss his—ring. I don't think there can be much doubt but that this guy's the new head hood replacing Mc-Cord."

"Who's the woman?" Anne Gilman asked. "McCord's widow?"

Holland shook his head. "McCord's wife died about a year ago. We don't have any idea who the woman behind the veil is."

He looked at Anne and at Cowper. "The reason I wanted to familiarize you with Clayton is that we may be close to a chance to bust the whole McCord operation, maybe including Clayton. I thought your office might want a riding D.A. to go along on the bust." "Riding D.A." was a police term for a representative of the D.A.'s office who accompanied the police to a crime scene.

"Tell me about the bust," Anne said.

Holland said, "We picked up a tip from an informer. The word is that tomorrow night the gang is transferring a load of stolen stuff from some place on Long Island where McCord had it stored until he could peddle it. The new site is a warehouse Clayton has picked out in the South Bronx. The informer says they're going to truck it in right after dark tomorrow night."

Anne put her fingers together and rested her arms on her elbows on the desk top. "And you know the location of this abandoned warehouse?"

Holland grinned. "We've already got it covered. We put an undercover surveillance team in place as soon as we got the tip yesterday. We plan to let them truck the stuff in, unload it, and bust them."

Anne said, "Sure, we want a riding D.A. along on the bust—me."

"I—" Holland started to say, and Anne cut him off.

"It's my decision," she said. "It's settled. I'll be ready to go tomorrow."

"Okay," Holland said. "You're the boss." He picked up the videotape. "I'm getting copies of this. You'll get one for your files."

He turned to go and noticed Callie Brinnin when she stood up to leave. Then he turned back toward Anne. "There is one other thing I should mention. Detective Brinnin here has volunteered to go undercover for us, starting tonight, at the Easy Street. She can try to keep an eye on Clayton for us if he shows up there."

Anne looked from Holland to Callie Brinnin.

Callie smiled, her teeth very white against her black skin. "I figure I can handle it all right given my protective coloration, it being Harlem and all."

Anne laughed. "I'm sure you can, Callie. I'm sure you can."

Charley Stenten sat on a bench a few feet into the entrance of Central Park near Fifty-ninth Street smoking a cigarette. The day was cloudless, the temperature below eighty degrees, a gentle breeze blowing. The horses and carriages that were always in the area to take customers for a ride through the park were being kept busy. Stenten knew he had no logical reason for doing what he was doing, and yet there he was, looking now and then toward Bettina Krager who sat two benches away, farther into the park. Part of the reason he was following her was that he wanted to study her so he could see if by any small sign from her demeanor he could intuit whether or not she had been capable of arranging the murder of her husband.

Once again he had tailed her from her building to the park as he had done two days earlier. It was the first time he had seen her since the night Frank Cavenaugh had told him there was some kind of connection between the man with the ponytail who had accosted her in front of the Plaza Hotel and Kenneth Shuba, the man found dead in the Krager apartment.

In those two days Stenten had read a steady stream of investigation reports on the Krager case sent to him by Cavenaugh. The reports detailed Cavenaugh's detectives' interrogation of the help regularly employed by the Kragers, the maid, the cook, the housekeeper, the Kragers' driver. None of them appeared to have any information to assist in the investigation. Stenten himself would do follow-up interviews with each of them if the NYPD Identification Section reported back that any of the four employees had a criminal record.

In addition, in the past two days, surveillance by Cavenaugh's detectives of the man with the ponytail had failed to reveal any contact between him and Bettina Krager.

Today, Bettina was wearing a sleeveless blouse, a straight skirt, low-heeled pumps, and a broad-brimmed straw hat that hid part of her face and most of her hair. She had brought with her a copy of the fashion publication *W*, Stenten observed, and appeared to be reading it. He did notice, however, that from time to time she glanced away from the paper to look at people approaching from one direction or another.

Stenten was momentarily distracted by two young people, a boy and a girl on skateboards who were revolving around and around directly in front of him before rolling away out of the park. When he turned back in the direction of Bettina he saw the man with the ponytail standing in front of her. The man was bent over her, saying something. Stenten could see her physically shrink back on the bench. Suddenly, the man grabbed her by the shoulders, pulling her toward him while she was trying to push him away, using both hands.

Stenten reacted without reflection, standing, walking quickly toward the two of them, and when he was close, calling out, "What's the trouble here? Ma'am, do you need any help?"

The man standing over Bettina spun around, his body rigid, his hands, released from her shoulders, clenched into fists. "Butt out!" he said to Stenten in a tight voice. "Mind your own business."

Stenten took a sidestep so that his back was to Bettina as he eased the top of his jacket back and let the man see the revolver in his shoulder holster. "Maybe I want to make this my business. Now, do you want to move along? Or do you want some serious trouble?"

The man backed away hurriedly, shaking his head, hands outthrust placatingly. "Okay. Okay. Take it easy. I'm out of here."

The man walked away, taking fast, jerky steps. Stenten watched him until he was out of sight in the park before turning to Bettina.

"Are you all right? He *was* annoying you, wasn't he?"

She seemed to have regained her composure although her face was pale.

"I—uh, yes, I'm all right. He—uh, he was, you know, panhandling. That's all it was."

Stenten nodded his head. "Sometimes they can be very persistent. It's a shame, too, people sitting, minding their own business"—he glanced at the paper on her lap—"reading *W* and some creep comes along, wanting a handout. You sure you're all right?"

"Oh yes." She stood. "And I do thank you. It's not true, is it, that New Yorkers never come to the aid of someone they think might be in trouble?"

They had fallen into step, walking out of the park.

"No, it's not true," Stenten said, keeping his tone light. "That's just an old wives' tale concocted by out of towners."

"That sounds like the statement of a native New Yorker."

Stenten smiled at her. "Transplanted, from New Jersey. How about you?"

"I was born and raised in Swarthmore, Pennsylvania. I've lived in Manhattan for about five years."

Stenten wanted to keep the conversation going. "You like it here?"

"Truthfully, I don't know where else I'd choose to live full-time. Like, other places might be nice to visit but I wouldn't want to live in any of them."

Stenten laughed. "If you feel that way, I think you'll

enjoy a comment I overheard the other night. I was in a restaurant, and as I was on my way out I heard one man say to the other, 'When you get right down to it, there are only two great cities in the world, the East Side of Manhattan and the West Side.' "

She laughed. They'd walked out of the park and on to Fifth Avenue. She seemed more relaxed.

Stenten decided to take a chance, hoping that what he said next wouldn't scare her off. "Look, I hope you'll understand. I'm going to have lunch and I hate to eat alone. Would you consider joining me? If you would, I'd like you to pick the place."

She looked at him for only a moment and said, "Yes. That would be very nice."

9

Callie Brinnin sat at the bar in the Easy Street Club in Harlem. The place wasn't very large, twenty tables, and a long bar. There were about a dozen people at the tables, six others, five men and a woman, at the bar. Callie had picked a spot at the upper end of the bar so she wouldn't have someone sitting on both sides of her, and two barstools to her left were empty. The customers made up what the new politics called "a mosaic," thirteen blacks, five whites.

The lighting was dim and the air was smoky. The bartender was a stocky black man who wore a white jacket and red bow tie. On the wall behind the bar was a mirror that extended from one end of the bar to the other.

Callie thought she looked knockout eye-catching, even if she did say so herself, in a short ivory dress with a matching jacket, light brown stockings, and patent leather pumps, pearl earrings, and a pearl necklace. She wanted to be noticed but not mistaken for a hooker and have to spend her time fending off horny johns.

So far, in the hour she'd been in the bar, there had been

only one minor incident. Right after she had first sat down and ordered a glass of white wine, one of the men sitting farther down the bar had got up and approached her. He was white, redheaded, not that old, but already had a beer belly. He was wearing a plaid jacket buttoned over a white T-shirt.

He leaned over the empty stool next to Callie and said, "Want some company, pretty woman? Buy you a drink?"

Callie smiled nicely as she shook her head. "Thank you, no."

"Uh-huh. I just thought I'd ask. You never know when someone might be lonely."

She thought it was over then but the next moment he'd unbuttoned his jacket and it fell open to reveal the front of his novelty T-shirt. On the front of the T-shirt was a drawing of a huge penis. Above the drawing were the words "Cover Me" and, below the drawing, the words, "I'm Coming In."

He made sure she'd seen the drawing and the words before he turned away, laughing, and returned to where he had been sitting, down the bar.

Callie decided the incident came under the heading of indecent adolescent exposure.

The bartender had been watching the brief encounter and he leaned over and filled Callie's wineglass. "On the house," he said. "And don't let that man scare you any. That's old Harold. He ain't exactly got dice that roll true. You know what I mean? But he's harmless. I'll see he won't bother you again."

Callie smiled. "Thank you. And for the wine, too."

"You just enjoy yourself. Anything you don't like, you tell me. The name's Dove."

"Thank you, again, Dove."

He nodded and went away.

The man hadn't scared her even enough for her to think of the .38 service revolver she carried in her handbag.

She sat for another quarter of an hour and suddenly the

doors to the street opened and a group of men came in, seven of them, all white. There were three men in front, one man behind them, and three more men walking in back.

Callie recognized the man walking alone, from the videotape: Roy Clayton. The other six men went straight to the back of the club and disappeared through swinging doors. Clayton came over to the bar and Dove rushed to greet him. The two men, heads close together, talked for a few minutes too far away for Callie to hear what they were saying.

Meanwhile, she saw the man named Harold leave the bar and also walk to the back of the club and through the swinging doors.

When Clayton finished his conversation with Dove, he turned and seemed to notice Callie for the first time. He looked straight at her and she looked straight back, half turned on the barstool so he could take her in from the legs up. He gave her a brief, tentative smile before he, too, headed for the back of the room and out of sight beyond the swinging doors.

Contact, Callie thought, and was satisfied.

Lieutenant John Holland had stayed late in his office at the 16th Precinct in midtown Manhattan. He was coordinating last-minute plans for the bust in the warehouse in the Bronx, to take place the next night. When there was a knock on the door, he shoved the plans into a folder and stuck the folder in his desk drawer. The office door opened and Detective Henry Grisham leaned his head into the doorway.

"See you for a minute, Lieutenant?"

Holland waved a beckoning hand. "Sure. I'm finished up here. What's on your mind? Sit down."

"What it is, Lieutenant, I heard you got a big raid coming up tomorrow night. I had to wonder why I'm not included."

Holland didn't answer right away.

Grisham, perched on the edge of the chair on the opposite side of the desk, looked like hell. His eyes were blood-shot, he needed a haircut, his Hawaiian shirt hanging out over the top of his trousers looked like it hadn't been washed in months.

Holland felt sorry for Grisham and what he answered, carefully, was, "I thought you might like to have a rest, Hank. I know you haven't been feeling up to par lately—"

Grisham said quickly, "A big bust like this could put some points on my service record if I'm included. I know you know that, so I wondered why I'm being shut out?"

"You want to talk about it, Hank, okay." Holland rubbed the bridge of his nose with a thumb and finger. "How's your personal life going?"

"Oh, that," Grisham said. "You know most of the details. It hasn't been easy since Betty divorced me. But I'm getting it together again."

"How long have you been living alone now?"

Grisham frowned as he thought and said, "Ten months. Yeah, almost a year. But what's that got to do—"

Holland cut him off. "Look, Hank, we're not going to get anywhere talking around your personal problems and your personal problems are affecting your performance in the department. Hell, you know that. I mean this subject isn't something that's suddenly materialized at this moment out of thin air. Why do you think a month ago you were ordered to talk to the police psychiatrist, what's his name?"

"Dr. Lyner," Grisham said. "So what's that got to do with now? I talked to him like I was ordered to. Has he been bad-mouthing me? Did he tell you something about me I ought to know?"

"What he told me was what his job calls for him to tell me: a general evaluation," Holland said, and added with some force, "I'm your commanding officer."

"All right, so what did he tell you about my personal life that now you think I need a rest?" Grisham paused, then said, "Not that I told him anything much anyway."

"It's not what he told me, Detective, it's what I can see for myself. You want to cut out all this bullshit and talk straight, we'll talk straight. You're drinking too much."

"Sure, sure, sure." Grisham nodded his head. "I'm drinking some off the job—"

"And on the job, too," Holland said quietly. "You think nobody notices. You think I don't notice. Come on, come on, Hank. You're fooling no one except yourself."

Grisham looked suddenly completely defeated. "Oh God, Lieutenant, I'm sorry, I'm sorry. You're right, I have been fooling myself. I have been drinking on the job some. I have been thinking nobody noticed. Drinking too much off the job too. What the hell am I doing with myself?"

Holland shook his head. "I don't know, Hank. You've always been a damn good detective. You wouldn't have been picked for the Task Force team if you weren't. I'd like to help you. But lately—" Holland let the words hang.

Grisham took out a cigarette and lit it, his hands trembling. He took a puff of smoke and exhaled it. "I guess it's showdown time, Lieutenant. I got to talk to somebody and I got to trust that you're the right somebody."

Holland waited, saying nothing.

Grisham hunched forward on the chair. "The divorce, living alone, that's been hard to handle. The drinking, too. It's all a part of what's been wrong with me. But it's not the real problem."

He took another drag on his cigarette and said, "It's—it's this girl." He stopped talking, his face sad.

"What girl?"

"A girl I met in a gin mill. She's barely in her twenties. Aggie Martin. She's young enough to be my daughter. And wild. She's all over me all the time. I never had it like that before, can you understand? And after the divorce and being lonely . . . But all the time I know Aggie's bad for me. Whatever's going on, she's like somebody's set a skyrocket under her and she's here, there, there, here, and taking me with her. Totally unpredictable. I don't think there's anything she wouldn't do if she got it into her head. I know she's bad for me, bad for herself. I know I got to forget her and . . . and . . . I can't get enough of her. I'm jittery all the time. I drink."

He held out a hand to Holland, sweat pouring down his face, "I'm *scared,* Lieutenant."

Holland came around from behind the desk. "Why don't you go wash your face, freshen up, and meet me downstairs."

Grisham looked worried. "And then what's going to happen?"

Holland said, "Just this one time we're going out for a couple of drinks. We're going to have a steak dinner. Then I'm going to drive you home. We're going to talk some more. We're going to work on setting things straight for you."

10

The temperature in midafternoon was ninety-five degrees. In the enclosed area of the backyard of the small two-story house on the west side in lower Manhattan near Tenth Avenue it felt another five degrees higher. The house was where, according to police reports, Lewis Bevvers had lived with Shirley Thomasson before she had disappeared.

Anne Gilman stood out of the way near the wooden fence that encircled the yard and watched as members of the NYPD Emergency Service Unit dug up the ground. Fine particles of dirt scattered in the air as shovels scooped the earth in an ever-widening hole and banked the soil in a pile against the fence opposite where Anne stood. Anne had come to the house directly after holding a press conference to announce that the D.A.'s office planned to seek indictments against a group of Asians in Chinatown who were suspected of smuggling aliens into Manhattan.

Here, earlier that day crewmen checking a reported ruptured sewer line at the rear of the house had, while digging down to the sewer pipes, uncovered the skeleton of a human hand. The crewmen had notified the NYPD and the Emergency Service Unit had come in to investigate.

As D.A., Anne could not be at every crime scene, of course, but she wanted to lend her presence whenever possible to the three current cases most important to her personally: the Bevvers case, the Krager killing, and the apprehension of the McCord burglary ring. As soon as Anne had been informed of the grisly discovery she and Assistant D.A. Rebecca Cohen had wanted to be present. Dr. Emmett Colterman, of the Forensic Science Lab, was there as well, standing by to preserve whatever bones were found for a later analysis.

One of the Emergency Service men had supplied Anne, Rebecca, and Colterman with gauze masks, worn by the men digging as well, and the proceeding looked like an eerie outdoor autopsy.

"Got something!" one of the diggers yelled out. He knelt, reached a gloved hand down into the hole, and lifted out a dirt-encrusted skull and held it up.

"Maybe, maybe," Anne said from behind the gauze mask, "we have the clinching evidence we need against Lewis Bevvers."

"From your lips to God's ear," Rebecca said.

Colterman took the skull and carefully placed it in a plastic evidence bag.

The digging went on for another three quarters of an hour without turning up any additional bones. As Anne and Rebecca left to return to the office, Colterman said, "I know what you want these bones to turn out to be, and I'm hoping I can prove it for you. But I want to caution you, as you may recall, that almost anywhere you choose to dig under the ground in Manhattan chances are you'll unearth a skeleton or two, some of them dating back to the days when the Indians were the only settlers here. It takes a lot of earth to cover all the bones of the human beings who have lived and died on this island."

Rebecca couldn't resist saying, "What you mean, Doc, is Manhattan was built on the bones of earlier generations."

Colterman, obviously a solemn man with little interest in small-talk remarks, answered, "Well yes, I suppose you could say that. For instance, I've always found it interesting that one of the greatest reservoirs of knowledge in the city, the main branch of the New York City Library at Fifth Avenue and Forty-second Street, was built above the site of what was once Potter's Field before the cemetery of unclaimed bodies was relocated to Hart Island."

When Colterman walked away, Rebecca whispered to Anne, "Boy! I guess he's what you'd call a real *bone*-head."

Anne had to laugh.

Eddie Leopold sat on the floor of the rotting tenement in the South Bronx, his eyes level with the bottom sill of the partially boarded-over window. Sweat oozed out from under his scalp and ran down his face, down his neck, soaking the top of his T-shirt. He wiped his hands on his grimy jeans, flicked the sweat from his eyes, and peered through the nightscope wedged into an opening between one of the boards nailed over the window and the sill.

"What time's it?" Leopold asked George Luther, who sat a few feet away from him in the darkness, his back braced against the wall, a two-way radio on the floor between his legs.

"Coming up on nine P.M."

Leopold grunted. His eye fixed to the nightscope, he scanned the rear façade of the abandoned warehouse across the alley. It, like the building he and George Luther were in, was falling apart. Over there low-watt lights were on inside a couple of the rooms behind the boarded-over windows. The rest of the rooms were dark. Through the 135-mm f/2.8

objective lens of the nightscope Leopold could see into the rooms that were dark.

Leopold and Luther, detectives with the NYPD Burglary Division, had been requested by Lieutenant Holland to assist in the night's operation against what was still known as the McCord gang.

George Luther said softly, "You know something, Eddie? When I was a kid growing up in Harlem and had this idea about being a cop I never thought I'd have to be working in places like this, worse than where I'd be if I had stayed in my old neighborhood."

"You think you got a complaint?" Leopold said jokingly. "I grew up in this neighborhood, broke my back to get out of it and into the police department—and here I am right back where I started."

"Well, I got to tell you, on second thought," Luther said philosophically, "if neither one of us had made it into the cops we'd both probably be over there with the bad dudes instead of here."

Leopold grunted. "You got a point there, all right, George. You know something else? You know why I like partnering with you?"

"Why's that?"

"Every time you get down about a situation, you right away think of something to cheer yourself up. It saves me a hell of a lot of time and talk trying to do it for you."

George Luther chuckled. "You noticed that about me, huh?"

"Yeah, I did, buddy." Leopold's bantering tone changed as he said quickly, "A big truck just turned into the alley and—hey—there's a car, looks like a Caddy, behind it."

Luther grabbed up the two-way radio and said tersely, "Eagle Eye to High Peak, come in!"

A second later Holland's voice came back on the radio, "I read you, Eagle Eye."

"Two vehicles coming into the alley. A truck and a car, a Cadillac, maybe."

Holland answered, "Got it. Stay put. Over and out."

John Holland, on the roof of a building at the end of the alley, used the radio again to communicate with the other members of the team who were in place at locations along the alleyway. "High Peak to all hands. Company's arrived. Maintain your positions until further orders."

Holland flicked off the radio and whispered to Anne Gilman standing beside him on the rooftop, "How do you like having a ringside seat right at the action?"

Anne answered, "Like my father always told me, 'If you can't go first-class, don't go.' "

Anne and Holland both had binoculars focused on the alley below. They saw the truck stop at a rear door to the warehouse under surveillance and the car, it was a Cadillac, stop behind the truck. The alley was in shadows but they could see figures emerging from the truck and the car, a couple of the figures hurrying into the warehouse while others were removing objects from the back of the truck and carting them into the building.

They watched until everyone who had been in sight below was inside. Holland used the two-way radio again, "High Peak to Totem Pole, move in. *Go*."

Now through the binoculars they could see other dark figures as they appeared from the ground floor of the building where Leopold and Luther were standing watch. The figures converged around the truck and the car, were lost from sight for a time, reappeared, and returned to the building where they had been waiting.

A voice came over Holland's radio: "Totem Pole to High Peak, mission accomplished."

"Good work," Holland answered, and said into the radio, "All hands! Zero hour! Watch yourselves! Let's see daylight!"

In the next moment the length of the alley and the front and back and both sides of the warehouse were lit up by blinding floodlights, powered by generators and set up on the roofs of various buildings surrounding the warehouse.

Simultaneously with the turning on of the floodlights, Holland lifted a bullhorn that carried his next words blaring out from one end of the alley to the other. "This is the police! I repeat, this is the police! You are surrounded! Stay inside with your hands on top of your heads! We're coming in! Any resistance and you will be shot!"

Down below, members of the police detail taking part in the raid streamed into the alley from the buildings where they had been hiding and, weapons in hand, charged through a side door to the warehouse.

At the same moment four of the men who had been inside the warehouse burst out of the back door into the alley. Two of the men ran for the truck. The other two men jumped into the Cadillac to back out of the alley. There was the roar of the car's engine. The car shot backward for several feet and stopped suddenly, the rear end digging into the asphalt surface of the alley as the car's back wheels—the lugs of which had been removed by the Totem Pole team—fell off, one wheel rolling zigzag by itself along the alley. The truck, in turn, was blocked from leaving the alley by the stalled Cadillac resting on its rear end.

Before the men in the car and in the truck could escape on foot they were ringed in by cops and handcuffed.

Watching from the rooftop above, Holland said to Anne, "Show's over. We can go down."

By the time they got down from the top of the building the alley was crowded with handcuffed suspects who had been brought out of the warehouse by the police as well as the ones who had been hauled out of the car and the truck.

"Be sure your men know that the suspects are to be informed of their rights before anyone is questioned," Anne warned Holland.

He nodded. "Let me see if we netted Roy Clayton." He moved away.

Anne looked on as a Department of Corrections van that had been waiting a couple of blocks away rolled into the alley and the handcuffed suspects were herded inside and driven away.

Holland returned, shaking his head. "We didn't nab Clayton. He must be playing the same game McCord played—never getting himself personally in any situation where he runs the risk of being arrested. Still, we'll put the ones we caught through the wringer. Maybe we'll get something so we can move against Clayton."

With all the suspects on their way to be questioned and booked, Holland gave instructions to reload the truck with the merchandise that had been transferred into the warehouse. Later would come the tedious job of establishing that the merchandise had been stolen.

11

Charley Stenten tried to make a joke as he sat in Anne Gilman's office, she behind her desk, and Stenten and Lieutenant Frank Cavenaugh sitting side by side, facing her. "What's this going to be, the third degree?" Stenten asked, trying to keep his voice light. "Maybe I should have a lawyer present to protect my rights."

Anne shook her head. She wasn't smiling. "Not funny, Charley. Frank wants to know what's going on between you and Bettina Krager. And so do I, for that matter."

"All right," Stenten said nonchalantly, as if the subject was hardly worthy of discussion, "so, Frank, the man you had following the creep with the ponytail saw me approach Bettina Krager in Central Park. Yeah, I talked to her, so what?"

Cavenaugh looked hard at Stenten. "According to the report I received, you did more than talk to her in the park. The two of you went merrily along out of the park to a fancy restaurant on Madison Avenue."

"Oh hell, Frank. Doesn't your guy have better things to do than tail me? I thought his assignment was to keep his eye on the creep?"

"His assignment is to find out the connection between him and her. You intruded yourself into the picture. And, incidentally, we've now got the guy's name, Peter Holmer. He's a free-lance photographer who makes whatever kind of living he makes as a cook in coffee shops. He and Kenneth Shuba were buddies, we hear."

"You haven't tried to question this Holmer yet?"

Cavenaugh shook his head. "We're going to wait a while and see if we can get a better fix on his relationship with her, Bettina. Now, what about you, what did you find out from her during your tête-à-tête?"

Anne's intercom buzzed. Anne said, "Hold it, guys." She flipped the intercom switch. "Yes, Jenny?"

"Lieutenant Holland's on the line. He wants to know if you can see him right away. He says it's important."

"Tell him yes, to come on over," Anne said. She looked at Stenten. "What about Bettina Krager? Did you learn anything? Does she know who you are?"

"She just thinks I'm some fellow who came to her rescue in the park, as far as I know. We didn't talk much about me. The truth is, I believe the only reason she went to have lunch with me was because she needed to talk to somebody and I happened to give her the opportunity."

Cavenaugh said, "So, let's hear what she had to say."

"It wasn't that she had any deep, dark secrets she wanted to reveal," Stenten said. "The kinds of things she mentioned were similar to the conversations people in New York sometimes have with cab drivers or even perfect strangers. You know? What's on their minds at the moment without really telling you anything meaningful."

"Did she know you knew who she was?" Anne asked.

"I don't know whether she knew or not before I told her I recognized her. I mean, I didn't see how I could avoid telling her that. After all, her picture's been splashed all over the place. I thought if I didn't say something she would get suspicious of me."

"Okay," Cavenaugh said, "once she knew you knew who she was, what did she tell you?"

Stenten waved a hand in the air. "Nothing you wouldn't have expected to hear. That the shooting of her husband had been a terrible tragedy. That she was still in shock. That she didn't know what she was going to do now. Stuff like that, mostly as if she was just thinking out loud."

Cavenaugh leaned toward Stenten. "Ask you a question, Charley?"

"Shoot."

"Do you plan on seeing her again? Or what? You think you can get her to tell you anything we need to know?"

"I don't have a plan," Stenten said. "After we had lunch I walked her back to her apartment building and we shook hands. I told her I might like to phone her sometime. She said she didn't know exactly what her plans were going to be. But I could try her. That was it."

Cavenaugh stood. "Let's keep coordinated. Soon as I know anything more about Peter Holmer, you'll hear."

"Same here," Stenten said, and started to stand but Anne motioned him back into his chair.

She said to Cavenaugh. "Take care of yourself, Frank."

"You, too. A.G., Charley."

Cavenaugh left.

As soon as he had closed the door behind him, Anne said, "Two things bother me about all this, Charley; I'll be honest with you."

"What's that?"

"One is that if you see Bettina Krager again and she doesn't know who you are and she tells you something that implicates her in her husband's murder we can't use it. In fact, if it turns out that she was involved and she's meanwhile told you anything that might incriminate her—and later she finds out who you really are—the whole case could be thrown out of court. Even if it can be proven she's guilty."

"I know that," Stenten said. "That hasn't happened yet.

If I do decide to talk to her again I'll tell her who I am before I let her tell me anything else. You said there were two things that bothered you. What's the second thing?"

Anne spoke carefully. "Frank indicated to me that he had the impression you might be resisting the possibility that she's involved in the murder. Something you said in a conversation you and he had."

"Oh hell," Stenten said. "He's referring to the night he came looking for me uptown to tell me about Shuba and this guy, Holmer, living in the same building. Right away Frank seemed to me to jump to the conclusion that that fact proved Bettina was involved. I wouldn't say I resisted the possibility, only the foregone conclusion."

Anne's intercom buzzed again and Jenny in the outer office said, "Lieutenant Holland and Detective Brinnin are here."

"Ask them to wait," Anne said, and turned her attention back to Stenten.

"Look, Anne," Stenten said quietly, "the last time you and I discussed the Krager case I was the one who said that I didn't want Homicide to shut the case down too soon as a simple breaking in and shooting. I was the one who theorized that she, Bettina, could have set the murder up. Remember?"

Anne nodded. "And I agreed with you. So why now does Frank get the idea you're backing away from your own theoretical possibility?"

"All I'm doing," Stenten said, "is expressing the same reservations in both instances. I've seen too often how it goes in the heat of an investigation. You know what I mean, the tendency to make a 'grounder' out of it."

Anne had worked with NYPD cops long enough to know what a "grounder" was, a term appropriated from baseball to mean an easy out, an easy solution to a crime. It was, as were all the terms incorporated into police jargon, a form of shorthand to save time in communicating.

"You've made your point, Charley. I know I don't have to say it but I will: As far as this office is concerned, you're running the Krager investigation. Do it as you see fit."

"Thanks, Anne." Stenten gave her a salute and started for the door.

"Charley, tell Jenny to send Lieutenant Holland in, please," Anne said. She leaned back in her chair until the door opened again and Holland and Callie Brinnin came in.

"I've got a new twist for you in the Roy Clayton case," Holland said. He placed a small portable recorder on Anne's desk. "Wait until you hear this. A wiretap."

He pressed the play button on the recorder. The tape recording was of two male voices, some of what they said blurred and indistinguishable:

"You guys get . . . word?"
"What word?"
". . . payoff."
"From who? What for?"
"The Big Man . . . thousand."
"Ten?"
"Yeah. Ten grand."
"You didn't say . . . for?"
"Anybody whacks . . ."
"Who?"
"The Irishman . . . ton. You know the party."
"Yeah. This . . . approved?"
"Everybody . . . man checked . . . agrees. Take him out now."
"I thought . . . protected."
"Before. With the old—the other one's his name. Not Clayton."
"Hey! I'll pass . . . word."

Holland pressed the off button and looked at Anne. "That's all we got. Intelligence picked it up from a tap they had on the phone at Salvatora's Café, the hangout of the Boglio family. The guy doing the talking about the payoff is Carmine Lutos, a soldier in the Boglio family. Intelligence

ID'd the other one as a soldier in the Franschetti family, nicknamed Bo-Bo. Not much question about what they're discussing. A hit."

Anne said, "And the Irishman is Roy Clayton."

Holland nodded. "From the tape I think we have to conclude that whatever alliance the McCord gang had with organized crime has ended with McCord's death. Also, that apparently all the families have approved the hit on Clayton."

Anne said, "And so now it's up to us to warn Clayton."

"Yeah. The commissioner concurred, now you; the commissioner informed the Feds, they concurred; Clayton is to be told. I'm going up to the Easy Street Club tonight to talk to him."

"Did we get anything on Clayton from the people we arrested at the warehouse?"

"Not yet," Holland said. "All of them were in and out on bail, none of them would talk. But Callie here's made a possible breakthrough that may help us down the line. Tell her, Callie."

Callie smiled at Anne. "The first night I was there at the club, Clayton eyed me over pretty good but didn't put a move on me. There were a lot of other guys up there that night. Clayton and the rest of them didn't spend much time in the front of the club. They sort of walked through and spent the rest of the night in a back room while I was there."

"Excuse me, Callie," Holland interrupted. "Let me explain to District Attorney Gilman that when we put the guys we arrested into a lineup before they got out on bail you were able to identify four of them from having seen them at the club that night."

"I did recognize them, yes."

Holland nodded at her. "Go on with the rest of your story."

"The night of the bust at the warehouse I went back to the club. The lieutenant and I didn't think I'd find Clayton there. We thought he'd be at the warehouse. But, as you know, he didn't go to the warehouse. In fact, he was at the club when I got there. This time he came onto me right away, insisted on buying me a drink, told me he was there because he particularly hoped I'd be there again. We moved from the bar over to a table and had dinner. He was very charming, I have to say. And acted like a perfect gentleman. He told me he'd like to see me again, get to know me better. I said I'd have to think about it. He didn't try to pressure me at all. He said he'd be at the club waiting for me if I decided I wanted to see him again. We left it like that."

Holland said, "I think it might be a good idea if Callie comes to the club tonight after I have my talk with Clayton. I think it's important that she keep her contact with him going."

Anne agreed. Then she had a thought: Wouldn't it be ironic if the reason Clayton hadn't gone to the warehouse was because he wanted to see Callie at the club that night?

12

There was still light in the evening sky when Anne left her office and walked out of the building. She'd requested Matt Slater to pick her up after work. She was meeting an old college roommate, Joan Metcalf, for drinks in midtown. As she came out on to the sidewalk, a man who had been waiting there approached her and said, "District Attorney Gilman?"

"Yes?"

"My name's Russell Cody, Sergeant, Internal Affairs Division." He held up his wallet so she could see his shield and ID card. He continued, "I think maybe I have some important information for you concerning one of your cases. Is there some place we can talk in private?"

"Well—" Anne looked around, then said, "I have a car and driver waiting. I can ask the driver to step out for a moment. We can talk in the car."

"Yeah, okay. This won't take long."

Anne walked to the car and opened the door. "Matt, would you mind leaving the car briefly. There's someone who wants to talk to me in private. Stay in sight, though."

"Sure thing, D.A. Gilman." Slater scrambled out of the car and walked a short distance away. Anne beckoned to Cody and they got into the backseat of the car.

Russell Cody was redheaded, heavyset, a neat dresser in a dark blue summer-weight suit, white shirt, blue tie with red stripes, black shoes.

"Thank you for talking to me," he said. "It's about that raid on the warehouse in the South Bronx. I saw the report on the news. From department scuttlebutt I've picked up I'd guess your real target was this new guy running the McCord gang, Clayton."

"And—" Anne asked.

"I know you missed him. I have reason to believe—coming out of a totally unrelated investigation I've been running—that Clayton was tipped off in advance of the raid."

"Tipped off? How?"

"If I'm right," Cody said, "this Clayton is getting inside information."

"Go on," Anne prompted.

"I think he's bought a cop, a detective."

Anne said quickly, "That's a pretty serious accusation, Sergeant."

Cody spread his hands. "Don't I know it! Why do you think I came to you? I don't have that much evidence but I do have certain information. If I take it directly into the department, I could be making trouble for myself. I tell you and you decide how you want to handle it. Maybe run an investigation out of your office."

"What's the information you have?"

Cody put a hand up to the knot of his tie and moved his head from side to side as if he were trying to make himself feel more comfortable.

"A couple of weeks back I was assigned to check on a certain detective. Nothing major. A matter of—well—erratic behavior. A difference in the degree of his job performance. There are guys in the department who keep an eye out for stuff like that, you can count on it. The next thing an order comes down to Internal Affairs: Nose around, see what's going on with the guy. When the order comes down they never tell you anything specific about the individual; they leave that up to you to find out. In this particular case, it was suggested maybe the guy was having a drinking problem."

Anne wasn't at all sure she wanted to hear what the sergeant was saying. But she also knew there was no way she could turn him off now without running the risk of appearing to have no interest in what Cody claimed to be vital information in one of her cases. She nodded to encourage him to continue.

Cody said, "I start tailing the guy after he finished work and, yeah, I find he's boozing it up plenty good. But that's not all I see. Worse than that he's got this crazy young chick he's mixed up with. You follow me?"

Anne frowned. "And you think that's why he'd sell information to Clayton? I don't—"

Cody said quickly, "There's more. See, this girl, I check on her too. She leads me to this club up in Harlem, you know about it, Clayton's hangout. Used to be McCord's place. Everybody knows about it. I see her talking to Clayton. The way I work it out is Clayton's the one put her onto the detective, turned him into passing information to Clayton. The thing is this detective is a member of the Organized Crime Task Force. Just the kind of pigeon Clayton would want."

Anne had trouble absorbing the words. "The Organized Crime Task Force itself?"

"Yeah," Cody said. "Lieutenant John Holland's group. The detective's name is Henry Grisham. That's about all I have to say. I thought you ought to know."

"You'd be willing to testify to what you've told me?" Anne asked.

Cody fiddled with his tie again. "As long as you understand I don't have any hard evidence. I guess what I think is maybe you should try to check into the whole business first, however you want to do it. A separate investigation from what I've found out, I would think."

Anne dismissed him then. "All right. I appreciate your coming to me. I'll be getting back to you."

"Sure thing." Cody got out of the car.

Matt Slater returned, got behind the wheel, and asked, "Everything all right?"

"It's okay, Matt."

On the drive to midtown, Anne thought over the story Sergeant Cody had told her. Was it possible Henry Grisham on the Organized Crime Task Force could be passing on confidential information to Clayton and nobody on the Task Force knew about it? She hated to even consider the implications but one thing was for sure: She'd have to find out, one way or the other.

She was meeting Joan Metcalf in the lobby of Thirty Rockefeller Plaza, headquarters of the National Broadcasting Company. Joan was the producer of a syndicated television interview program, *Personality Profiles*. When they'd made the date to meet for drinks, Joan had said she had business at NBC that day and asked Anne to meet her there in the lobby.

After Matt Slater dropped her off and she told him she'd see him in the morning, she went into the lobby. Joan wasn't there yet. Anne waited at their usual meeting spot, just inside the entrance directly under the mural of a figure, a nude male, entitled *Time*. Anne remembered with amusement the first time years before, when Joan in a phone call had identified the meeting spot in the lobby and Anne had repeated what she thought Joan had said, "Under the clock?" Looking up now at the mural, Anne remembered Joan's correction, "*Under the crotch, under the crotch.*" Joan had explained that when Anne saw the mural she'd understand the reference, a play on words used by people who worked in the building.

Anne waited there for a few minutes, watching people

hurrying past, most of them headed out of the building at this hour, a few entering, looking around, probably tourists, and then there was Joan coming from the bank of elevators behind the lobby, walking fast as always.

Joan Metcalf had silver-blond hair, every hair in place, pulled back in a tight chignon, startling green eyes, a smooth creamy complexion. Always, Anne thought Joan looked chic in the simplest off-the-rack outfits. Today she wore a lime sheath dress, green earrings, a green beaded necklace.

Joan hugged her. "Were you waiting long?"

"Just got here."

"You look great. How about we have drinks at 'Twenty-one'? I could use a chilled Chablis."

"Sounds fine."

As they walked the couple of short blocks to "21," Joan talked about her television show. *Personality Profiles,* running on one of the small local TV stations, was up for renewal at the end of the year. She was making the rounds of the networks, hoping to sell the program to prime time.

"Not encouraging so far," Joan said. "I think the problem is that talk shows are almost talked out. I must admit that I myself never watch any of them except my own show. I mean, by this time all of us must have heard everything anyone has to say on TV at least twice. And, at that, most of it is junk talk."

She laughed. "Listen to me go on, biting the hand that turns the TV dial that feeds me. Shameless!"

Anne laughed too. "Joan, you haven't changed a day since we used to sit around the room at school bitching about how unfair the professors were and all the while getting straight A grades. It's the same thing, isn't it?"

Joan looked at Anne and winked. "Kid, it's good to know my moral center is still holding."

In "21" they sat at a table in the bar under the assortment of bright-colored toys suspended from the ceiling and drank wine.

"So tell me in general terms," Joan asked, "how the battle between the good guys and the bad guys is going?"

Anne shrugged and said lightly, "About all I can tell you is what you already know; both sides are keeping busy."

Joan took a sip of wine. "You know my show is always there for you to come on if there's ever anything you want to say. I don't mean that as any form of pressure, you surely know, even if I think it would boost the show's ratings. It's just that it's occurred to me that sometimes you may have something to say outside of a Q and A press conference."

"I understand," Anne said. "Who knows? There may come a time. I appreciate the offer."

Joan brushed the palms of her hands together. "Now that we've gotten all of the frivolous stuff about ourselves out of the way, let's talk about serious matters. How's your love life? Or are you as reticent to reveal anything about your sexual activities as you were when we were roommates?"

Anne laughed. "I'll tell you the same thing as I told you then; there's someone, yes."

"Lord! Not the same someone, I hope."

"Of course not. A present someone."

"But that's all you're saying?"

"What more is there to say? If you know there's someone then you know all the rest of it." Anne leaned forward and said mischievously, "As for the details—on the bed, on the floor, on the table, in the car, on the beach, in the shower, in the tub, standing up or lying down, from any direction, in any position, it feels good. As you know from your own similar experiences. Does that answer your question?"

Joan burst out laughing. "Boy! You appear on the show and tell the public all that and it'll be something they haven't heard at least twice before on TV."

Anne was laughing too. "At least not from a district attorney."

"I guarantee the ratings would go through the roof!"

Anne said, "And that's not all that would go through the roof."

They both laughed.

A few minutes after 8:00 P.M. Holland walked into the Easy Street Club. He spotted Roy Clayton sitting alone at a table, a drink in front of him. Holland walked directly to Clayton, noting on the way that there were four people sitting at the bar, three black men and a white woman, six other people at tables, all six black, three men and three women.

At Clayton's table, Holland said, "Mr. Clayton, I wonder if I could have a word with you? I'm Lieutenant John Holland, New York City Police Department."

Clayton looked down at Holland's identification and then looked up. His expression was impassive. "What can I do for you?"

Holland spoke quietly even though the other people in the club were sitting a distance away. "I have some information I've been ordered by my superiors to pass on to you. It's a matter concerning your safety."

Clayton lifted a hand palm up. "Fine. Tell me." He motioned to a chair.

Holland sat down. "Recently the police department came into possession of certain information indicating you may possibly be in some danger."

"What is all this?" Clayton demanded. "What danger?"

"Take it easy," Holland said. "We have reason to believe that there are individuals who would like to see you dead."

"Is that a fact," Clayton answered sarcastically. "And you're sitting there trying to tell me that the police department sent you to find me and tell me this? You guys sure must not be busy if you have nothing better to do."

"Listen, Clayton"—Holland's voice was hard—"it's the policy of the police in this city, if it has such knowledge, to notify any citizen it suspects might be in danger from another individual or individuals."

"Who? Who is this individual, or individuals, that want me dead? And why? If you know so much."

"There's no way I can tell you specifically who the individuals are," Holland said. "As to why, according to what we've learned, they, they seem to think you have inherited—whatever—from Terrence McCord. According to what we hear, they, they have decided whatever arrangement existed as far as McCord was concerned is ended. To put it bluntly, they want you out of the way."

Holland saw the muscles in Clayton's jaw tighten, and his face seemed to darken. The look of a black Irishman, Holland thought, with a temper in check somewhere inside him.

Clayton's answer, however, was offhand: "Somebody'd have to be crazy to want to kill me just because McCord left me this club."

"Have it your way." Holland made a move as if to leave.

"Another thing," Clayton said, "if the police have information that somebody's planning to kill me, why don't they arrest them?"

Holland was standing. "We will. We will. The trouble is you may be dead by then, for all the good it'll do you."

Holland turned and walked out of the club. He saw that Callie Brinnin had come in and was sitting at the bar, her back turned to him.

Outside, Holland crossed the street and walked down the block for a few paces to a phone booth near where he'd parked his car. From the phone booth he could see the entrance to the Easy Street. He dialed Anne Gilman's home phone number. She answered on the third ring. He told her he'd talked to Clayton. When he'd finished the account, she said it was urgent that she see him as soon as possible, that night, that something had come up he needed to know. It was very important.

"Callie's still inside the club," he said. "Unless I miss my guess Clayton's not going to be in much of a mood to schmooze with her tonight. After what I told him he's going to have other things on his mind. If he leaves, Callie's not likely to stick around long. I'd like to hang around and drive her home. Then I'll come to your place."

Anne said she'd be waiting.

Holland hung up the phone and went to sit in his car.

Inside the club, Callie had been watching Clayton in the mirror as he had gone to a phone booth in the rear of the room after Holland left. She saw him dial several numbers, speak briefly, hang up, and dial again.

The bartender, Dove, had come over to Callie once and wanted to give her another glass of wine. She'd told him maybe later. Mostly to make conversation with him so he wouldn't notice she was trying to watch Clayton, Callie asked about a piano now sitting in the front part of the bar that had not been there on her previous visit.

"There's entertainment two nights a week here," Dove told her. "Other times the piano's in the back room. Later tonight a gal sings and plays. People in the neighborhood come in, the place's jammed. Used to be in the old days sometime in the fifties, they tell me, people would come from all over to listen to the blues singers here. They say some of them that went on to sing at the Apollo Theatre sang here first. Old Mr. McCord, used to own the place, died not long ago, they say he had a liking for blues music."

A couple of new bar customers came in then and Dove moved away to serve them.

Now Callie saw Clayton come out of the phone booth and head for the front door, walking fast. Clayton almost passed her by, saw her, and turned back.

"I was hoping I'd see you again," he said. "Right now I've got some business elsewhere. You'll come back again?"

Callie smiled. "Sure."

She watched Clayton leave and finished her wine. She put some money on the bar and stood up. Dove came hurrying back.

"Don't you want to hear the entertainment?"

"Another time, Dove," she told him. "I'll be back."

"I'm sure counting on it," Dove said.

She walked out and heard her name being called. She saw Holland across the street waving to her. She went over and got into his car, glad she didn't have to take the subway downtown and home to Queens.

Anne had ready a stiff drink of Jack Daniel's for Holland when he came into the house. "I thought you might need this," she said, handing him the glass, "after your session with Clayton and before you hear what I have to tell you."

She was in lounging pajamas and a robe and was bare-foot. She sat on the sofa, her legs crossed under her, and watched Holland drink half the Jack Daniel's before he put the glass down on the coffee table.

"That helped," he said.

He walked to the sofa, leaned over, a hand on either side of her against the sofa cushion, and kissed her, her arms going around his neck, holding him tight before releasing him.

"And that," he said, moving to sit next to her, "helped even more."

Smiling, he cupped her chin with his hand. "You look so solemn. Whatever it is, we'll fix it. Tell me."

She told him about her conversation with Russell Cody.

He kept shaking his head as she talked.

"No way is what Cody told you true," Holland said when she'd finished talking. "I know Hank Grisham. He's had some personal problems, I'm aware of them, but there's no way he'd sell out the department. Not for love or money."

Anne looked at him searchingly. "Can you be that sure? Sergeant Cody seemed convinced of what he was saying. He said he's willing to testify, meaning to a grand jury. He'd know that's where I'd take the investigation, that the matter's too big for the police department, even Internal Affairs.

Would he do all that if he thought there was a chance he might be wrong?"

Holland said patiently, "It's the job of detectives in Internal Affairs to ride herd on malfeasances within the department. Sometimes there are cops who are corrupt; I.A.D. investigators are there to police the police, you know that. I have to believe Cody *believes* what he told you is true—"

"But?"

"But, in the case of Hank Grisham, I already knew he was drinking, I already knew he was mixed up with some kooky girl. What Cody has come up with are the same two things I already knew—and he's jumped to a conclusion I'd have to see proven before I'd believe it." He shook his head. "What I think is that Sergeant Cody has put two and two together and come up with five."

"Speaking as D.A.," Anne said, "I don't like sitting on this for too long. If it turns out that Sergeant Cody was right and he brought me the facts and I didn't act on them, it could create some serious problems."

"What I'm asking is that we cover for Hank only until I see him and talk to him for myself. I think I, we, all of us, owe him that. If word gets around of what Cody suspects and even if Hank's proven innocent, it'll end his career. After I've talked to him if I'm not completely satisfied, we'll throw Hank to a grand jury and move against him. Okay? Is it a deal?"

Anne was still doubtful but she said, "It's a deal."

Holland picked up his drink and smiled at her. "Now that that's out of the way, the only serious question left is do I stay over tonight?"

"Well," Anne hesitated, then thought, why not. "Since tomorrow's Saturday I see no reason why you shouldn't."

Charley Stenten had been sleeping fitfully for about an hour when the ringing of the phone next to his bed brought him fully awake.

"Hello," he said. "What is it?"

"Charley, this is Frank Cavenaugh. Are you awake?"

"For Christ's sake, Frank, I am now."

"Good. So am I. With the weekend coming up I thought I should tell you tonight there's been a new development in the Krager case."

Stenten held the receiver to his ear and rubbed his head with his other hand. "Yeah?"

"I just listened to a wiretap we put on the phone in the Krager apartment—"

Stenten, surprised, asked, "You got a tap on the phone?"

"We got a court order, it's kosher," Cavenaugh said. "Anyhow, the point is the tape picked up a call a little while ago from that creep, Peter Holmer, to Bettina Krager. It told us everything we need to know about their connection. We've got it all recorded. Can you hear me all right, Charley?"

"I hear you."

"He warns her in the call to stop stalling, meet him on Sunday with the money or he's going to tell the police everything he knows about the murder of her husband. How you like that?"

"He said all that, huh?"

"We've got it word for word. I'm having a copy of the recording made for you and A.G. to hear on Monday. Meanwhile, I've got a pickup order out on Holmer. We'll bring him in for questioning as soon as we find him. We'll talk to him first before we bring her in. You'll get the credit on this one if it hangs together. Go back to sleep."

"Appreciate the call, Frank."

Stenten hung up the phone, got out of bed, and went into the living room. He sat, thinking about what he was going to do or not going to do now.

13

Anne always looked forward to the weekends she didn't have to work. Saturdays she reserved for herself alone during the day. She did her shopping then, alternating between buying groceries one week and clothes shopping the next. On most Saturdays Holland picked her up and they drove to Connecticut where he had a small house on a lake not far from Greenwich. Saturday nights they drove to a restaurant or inn nearby, had dinner, and frequently went to see a movie. Afterward, they would pick up *The New York Times* and the *Daily News*. Sundays they slept late, then read the papers, often spending the day in the house, with Anne fixing a big breakfast and a late lunch before they returned to Manhattan in the early evening.

On this Saturday morning, a day for grocery shopping, Anne left her house about eleven. She followed a routine that took her around the neighborhood, to the local supermarket for groceries, to the fish store, the meat shop, the bakery, and the Korean fruit and vegetable stand. She took her purchases home and went back out to treat herself to brunch in the Carlyle Hotel on Madison Avenue.

She particularly enjoyed summer Saturdays in the city. Traffic moved at a more leisurely pace. There were fewer people on the streets, strolling instead of rushing, doing errands, shopping, or just window-shopping. Too, there were the young men and women in tennis outfits, carrying their rackets, headed for the courts in Central Park or John Jay Park on the East Side; and the families and children coming from the Lexington Avenue subway on their way to the swimming pool also at John Jay Park.

As often, Anne had an excellent brunch—a plate of assorted seafood delicacies. She had just finished and was drinking a second cup of coffee when her beeper signal sounded, startling the other diners around her. She quickly cut off the sound, paid her check, and went out to the lobby to a phone booth, where she dialed the readout numbers on the beeper.

A voice at the other end of the line said, "Who's this?"

She didn't recognize the voice.

"You called me," she said.

"D.A. Gilman?"

"Yes."

"Boy! Am I glad I reached you! This is Detective Fred Myler, you know, one of Lieutenant Holland's men on the Organized Crime Task Force—"

"I know who you are," Anne said. "What's the problem, Myler?"

"You haven't heard? About last night, today?"

"Heard what?"

"There's been a lot of stuff going down the last twenty-four hours. They can't reach the lieutenant. I think you ought to be here," Myler said.

"Where?"

"You know the NYPD 'junk car lot'—"

"I know," Anne said. It was the police name for the parking lot in lower Manhattan where vehicles involved in a crime were taken to be examined and searched.

Myler said, "Well, I think you ought to come here right away."

"I'll get a cab and be there as quickly as I can," Anne said, and hung up the phone.

There were rows and rows of cars lined up behind the chain link fence of the junk car lot. Most of them would in time, usually after thirty days, and after they had been searched and examined, be shipped to the car pound in College Point, Queens, to be auctioned off. Myler stood with Anne beside one of the cars parked at the front of the lot. The car, a new Cadillac, had all the windows and the windshield shot out. All four doors stood open and the front seat was splattered with blood.

"This was the first one that was found, early this morning by a prowl car, up off the West Side Highway near the George Washington Bridge. It wasn't until the local precinct up there ran a check on the registration that headquarters was informed. The car was owned by Joey Rocco, you know, belongs to the Boglio crime family. Headquarters ordered the precinct to bring the car here and called me and were calling the other Task Force people. I just heard they located Lieutenant Holland. They said he's on his way here."

"How about the owner of the car?" Anne asked. "Rocco? Any trace of what became of him?"

"Nothing on him." Myler shook his head. "The squad car guys who found the Cadillac say they searched all around the area up there and there was not only no trace of him but no blood around outside the car to indicate he got out alive."

"As for the other car"—Myler turned and motioned with his thumb at a Buick parked near the Cadillac—"it was found just before noon today in Central Park by one of the mounted patrolmen, doors open, keys in the ignition. No bloodstains but the registration papers were in the glove compartment. When the Central Park precinct reported to headquarters that it had found the car and it belonged to Albert Turno, a soldier in the Rigletto family, headquarters directed that the car be brought here."

Anne glanced at the members of the police forensic team who were examining the inside of the Buick.

"As for where Turno disappeared to—" Myler shrugged. He rubbed his head and said, "And there's one more thing, too. The police in Brooklyn received a phone call a couple of hours ago that four masked men broke into the home of Louis Ugo, *consigliere* of the Tennelli family, in Brooklyn Heights. The four men tied up the family and took Ugo away. So what it looks like is we got some kind of warfare going on between three crime families."

Anne saw Myler smile suddenly as he looked past her and, with obvious relief in his voice, said, "Here comes the lieutenant."

Holland had parked his unmarked car a couple of yards away, inside the fence, and approached Anne and Myler, nodding as he came.

"I've been in touch with headquarters by radio," Holland said. "They told me some of what's been happening. Fill me in."

Myler and Anne walked with Holland to the two cars that had been brought to the lot and Myler repeated the information he'd told Anne.

When he'd finished, Holland said, "That son of a bitch!"

Myler was puzzled. "Who?"

"Clayton. Roy Clayton. He has to be the one who did this, all of it." Holland quickly told Myler of his visit to the Easy Street Club the night before and added, "I'll give him this, though, he sure moved fast to take action once he knew there was a contract out on him."

Myler looked disbelievingly. "You really think a putz like Clayton would go up against all the mob families?"

"Yeah, I really do think so."

Holland looked at Anne. "Your opinion?"

"I think it's possible, yes. If he's not that experienced

about how these things go, and if he thought he had no other choice."

Holland said, "He may not be such a putz, either."

"How do you mean?" Myler asked.

Holland looked toward the two cars and back again. "Think about it. A gangland killing, the usual method is to leave the body there to be seen, bullet-riddled, a warning that it was a cold-blooded execution. Clayton, if he's the one, has changed the rules. Why else would the bodies be removed? I tell you he's not out to kill them; he's out to spook them as well."

Anne said thoughtfully, "There may be another angle to this method as well. It would be harder to prove the murders if the bodies aren't found."

Holland dismissed the idea. "I wouldn't worry too much about that. It's not that easy to dispose of a carload of bodies, especially once all the law enforcement agencies are alerted to be on the lookout for them. I'll give you odds that within the next twelve to twenty-four hours the harbor patrol or somebody else'll dredge them up."

Holland's words proved to be wrong. By Monday morning when Anne got to her office none of the bodies of the three men who had disappeared, Rocco, Turno, Ugo, had been found. To add to the mystery two more gangland members had turned up missing sometime between Saturday night and Sunday night.

On Saturday night a soldier in the Turella family, Dino Capri, was grabbed off the street in front of his house just after he'd parked his car at the curb. Capri lived in Hoboken, just across the river from Manhattan. Four men leapt out of a station wagon, hauled Capri into the vehicle, and sped away. There were neighbors sitting outside all around Capri's house. Nobody could give a description of the four men or a license plate number on the station wagon.

The following afternoon Nicholas "Slick Nick" Dolayga,

captain in the Boglio family, was drinking coffee with his bodyguard in Salvatora's Café in Little Italy. Six men entered the café, three through the front door, three through the back door. The bodyguard was killed where he sat with four shots through the back of the head from a 9-mm Taurus PT99. The six men lifted Dolayga bodily, carried him out to a waiting car, and drove away, leaving the dead bodyguard behind. Again, such witnesses as there were could provide no information on what the six men looked like or the car they used.

All three New York City newspapers were on Anne's desk. All carried front-page stories with headlines that were a variation on WHO'S KILLING THE MOB?

Jenny had greeted Anne with, "The media people have been calling every two minutes. They want a statement on what's happening with all the shootings and disappearances."

"Tell them there'll be a press conference later. We'll let them know."

John Holland had left a message that he'd been called to a meeting with the police commissioner and would be calling for an appointment later.

Frank Cavenaugh had sent over a tape recording of a telephone tap placed on Bettina Krager's phone. Charley Stenten hadn't come into the office yet and Anne decided she'd wait for Stenten to be present before she listened to the tape.

Dr. Colterman of the Forensic Science Lab was waiting outside Anne's office to report on the human skull that had been recovered from the yard outside the house where Lewis Bevvers had lived with Shirley Thomasson. Anne had kept Colterman waiting until Rebecca Cohen arrived for work and Colterman and Rebecca came into Anne's office together, Colterman carrying a huge white box that looked like it could have contained an enormous wedding cake.

Colterman placed the box in the center of Anne's desk

on top of the newspapers and announced, "Folks, you're going to be surprised at the news I have for you."

It was clear that the doctor was enjoying his moment as he carefully removed the skull from a plastic bag and then lifted out a large manila envelope.

"Just tell us," Rebecca said, "have you identified the skull?"

Colterman was removing a sheet of paper from the manila envelope. "Almost certainly, yes."

"And it's Shirley Thomasson's skull, yes?" Rebecca asked impatiently.

Colterman was not to be hurried. "Let me show you an amazing piece of work."

As Anne and Rebecca looked on silently, Colterman laid the sheet of paper on the desk. On it was a sketch of a woman's face.

"From such facts as we were able to come by, based on medical records of the victim Thomasson, and a forensic examination of the skull itself, we were unable to determine whether or not this was her skull."

Rebecca started to say something but Colterman held up a hand. "However, I next sought the help of one of the expert police artists to see if it was possible for him to try to reconstruct in a drawing what the face might have looked like before death." Colterman held up the skull. "The artist first took photographs of the skull and projected those photographs onto a sketch pad. He then tried to re-create a face working from the sockets where the nose, mouth, and eyes were. We then compared the various sketched likenesses with photographs of the victim obtained from police files."

The doctor took a black-and-white photograph from the envelope and placed it next to the sketch drawn on the sheet of paper. "Look carefully now," he said, moving a finger from the sketch to the photograph. "Granted that there are dissimilarities between the two, the hair for instance, which the artist had to guess at, the lips, you can clearly see the remarkable resemblance between sketch and photograph."

Anne asked quickly, "The artist hadn't seen the photograph before he rendered the sketch?"

"No, no, he hadn't. But you haven't heard all of it yet."

Anne was frowning. "All right. What?"

Colterman pointed to the photograph. "This isn't the victim Shirley Thomasson."

Rebecca appeared bewildered. "I don't understand what you're saying!"

"When the sketches were completed," Colterman said, "I compared them to the photograph of Shirley Thomasson. There was no discernible likeness between the two."

Rebecca shook her head. "You've lost me, Dr. Colterman."

"I felt the same way," he said. "But then I had another idea and I went back to the police photo files and discovered the picture you see there. The photograph, with the remarkable resemblance to the artist's sketch, is a photograph of Lucille Etherton who was, as I understand, suspected to be an earlier victim of this man, Lewis Bevvers."

Anne and Rebecca looked at one another.

Rebecca said softly, "The dirty son of a bitch killed Lucille Etherton before he moved in with Shirley Thomasson and then buried Etherton's body in Thomasson's backyard."

"Good Lord!" Anne said in a whisper, her voice shaking, "And a jury has acquitted Bevvers of the murder of Lucille Etherton!"

14

When Charley Stenten got to the office that morning, late, there was a note on his desk that D.A. Gilman wanted to see him. He called Anne's office. Jenny Corso told him Anne was in a meeting and couldn't be disturbed. Jenny said she'd let him know when the meeting ended.

Stenten had picked up a container of coffee on his way from the subway to the office. He lit a cigarette, drank some coffee, and dialed Frank Cavenaugh at his precinct. He had to wait a while before Cavenaugh came on the line. Stenten asked if the police had picked up Peter Holmer yet.

"We've got his apartment staked out," Cavenaugh said. "No sign of him so far."

"How about Bettina Krager? I assume you've had surveillance on her. Did she meet Holmer on Sunday?"

"We've been watching her building, as well as his, around the clock. We know she's been inside because we still have a tap on her phone and she's made personal calls from time to time. We don't know whether Holmer's in his apartment or not. But there's been no call from him to her or vice versa. Did you listen to the tape I sent over?"

"Not yet," Stenten said. "Gilman's been tied up in a meeting. I'm waiting to see her. You'll let me know if there are any new developments?"

"You'll hear."

Stenten hung up the phone and leaned back in his chair to finish his cigarette and coffee. Damn! He wanted to help Bettina Krager and he didn't honestly know whether it was because of his personal feelings for her or because, instinctively, he couldn't bring himself to believe she was capable of arranging her husband's death. What's more, he couldn't think of how he might see her again or even contact her now that Cavenaugh had her phone tapped and had her under surveillance around the clock. If he made any attempt to call her or see her Cavenaugh would know. If he did either he'd better have a good reason.

His thoughts were interrupted when Jenny on the phone told him Anne was free and wanted to see him.

He was surprised when a few minutes later he walked into Anne's office. She was sitting behind her desk, her face somber. She didn't waste time in greeting him. She said only, "Frank Cavenaugh sent over a tape recording of a tap on Bettina Krager's phone. It's of a call she received from Peter Holmer."

"I know," Stenten said. "Cavenaugh told me about it."

Anne had already put the tape into the recorder beside her desk. She pressed the button.

"Hello?"

"Is this Bettina Krager?"

"Who is this?"

"You know who I am . . ."

"If you don't tell me who you are I'm going to hang up!"

"I already told you my name; Peter Holmer, remember?"

"I told you I have nothing to say to you."

"Hang on! You'd better listen, lady! I told you what I wanted! You'd better see that I get it! You meet me Sunday. You know where. And you'd better have the money or I'm going to tell the police everything I know about your husband's murder!"

The tape ended with the click of the phone. Anne leaned over and turned off the recorder.

Stenten waited for Anne to speak.

When she said nothing and started rewinding the tape, Stenten said, "I guess I'd have to say this adds a different slant to Richard Krager's murder."

Anne looked at him as if for a moment she'd forgotten he was there.

Stenten added, "I just talked to Frank before I came in. He says they're looking for Peter Holmer. They want to see what they can get out of him before they do anything about her."

"Yes," Anne said. "That would be the next logical step."

Stenten could see that her mind was elsewhere. He supposed it had to do with the gangland violence over the week-. end. He said, "I'll keep behind Frank."

"Do that." Anne nodded.

Jenny Corso buzzed in on the intercom, "Lieutenant Holland is here."

"Send him in," Anne said.

Anne looked at Stenten. "It's one of those days."

"I know," Stenten said. "I read the papers this morning."

As Stenten left he and Holland passed one another in the doorway and spoke, nodding.

"Lieutenant."

"Lieutenant."

Holland closed the door and turned. He said to Anne, "A good man, Charley Stenten."

"Yes, he is," Anne agreed. And then, "How'd it go with Clarkson?" Donald Clarkson was the police commissioner.

"Just as you might imagine," Holland said, pulling up a

chair. "He wanted to know what the hell was going on? The same question the newspapers are asking: Who's killing the mob? Did we have any idea? I told him what we suspected."

"And—"

"And he wanted to know what we were going to do about it. And when we were going to do it."

"I've been asking myself the same question," Anne said. "Did any bodies turn up anywhere yet?"

Holland grimaced. "I think I was premature in my judgment on that one. I did say, remember, that if it was Roy Clayton's handiwork, maybe it was part of his plan to dispose of the bodies so they wouldn't be found. Remember I said it sure as hell would spook the rest of the organized crime families."

"What about Clayton? Has he been seen since all this started? Has Callie Brinnin been back to the club?"

"She was there Saturday night, and last night. There was no sign of him. She said she didn't see anyone else there who looked like they might be a part of Clayton's gang, either."

"Are you going to keep sending her back there?"

"For a couple of more nights, at least," Holland said.

"All right. I'll tell you what I plan," Anne said. "I'm going to convene a secret grand jury, ongoing. We'll present them with what we have: the chain of evidence, starting with Terrence McCord, and going on from there with what we've gathered on Roy Clayton."

Holland agreed. "Good idea."

"We probably don't have enough yet to get a vote of indictment. But we'll have a grand jury in place and we'll keep presenting them with evidence as it develops."

Anne made notes on a sheet of paper, saying as she wrote, "I'll want you to be the key witness. I'll need Callie to testify, and the officers who were at the scene when Rocco's car and Turno's car were found. And we'll give them the videotape you made at McCord's funeral and the wiretap where the hit against Clayton was discussed."

"I'll be ready." Holland nodded.

"This week," Anne said.

Holland nodded again.

Anne pushed the sheet of paper aside. "Now then, what about Henry Grisham?"

She and Holland had not been together the day before in Connecticut.

"Yeah." Holland was clearly unhappy about what he had to say next. "I went looking for him Saturday night and yesterday. He lives in a studio apartment in Astoria. He wasn't home. I found the bar where he's been hanging out, usually with his girlfriend. Nobody in the bar's seen him or her for the past couple of days. And he didn't show up for work this morning."

"I don't like it," Anne said.

Holland held up a hand. "I left word around to be notified if he turned up at the apartment or the bar or in his neighborhood. I want a few more days before we blow the whistle on him. I think he just needs a little time to pull himself together."

"You don't think he's skipped out?"

"No way! He just wouldn't do it. Please, Anne, a few more days."

"A few more days—and that's it," she said firmly.

"Agreed." Holland looked at her carefully. "Something else is bugging you."

She told him about the visit from Dr. Colterman and the identification of Lucille Etherton's skull.

Holland, trying to be helpful, said, "You'll nail Bevvers in the next trial, baby."

"I suppose," Anne said, "but do you know how it makes me feel that he got away, free forever, with a murder we'd surely have proved if we'd found the skull before he was tried?"

"It happens. You just have to hang in there."

"Oh I know. I know."

Holland put up two fingers to his lips, leaned over the desk, and pressed his fingers to her lips. "Love you," he whispered, and left the office.

Holland arranged for Callie Brinnin to be driven to Harlem in a squad car that night, to save her a subway ride. It was about eight P.M. when the car dropped her off a block away, around the corner, from the Easy Street Club.

She slung the strap of her handbag over her shoulder, holding the bag tight under her arm, and looked around carefully to see that no one had taken notice of her getting out of the squad car. Walking rapidly to the corner, she turned and saw that the club was dark. She was puzzled. Then she saw that there was a white sheet of paper taped to the inside of the front door. She went closer to the door and read the message written in black ink: CLOSED UNTIL FURTHER NOTICE.

She backed away from the door and started walking up the block toward the downtown subway; a wasted trip, she thought disgustedly. As she approached a car parked midway in the block the door opened and Roy Clayton stepped out, facing her and making a small bow.

"Good evening," he said, smiling. "I was hoping you might come back tonight. Dove, the bartender, told me you'd been in the last couple of nights. Last time I saw you I told you I hoped I'd see you again. Remember?"

"I do remember," Callie said.

"So now is when I see you again." He held the car door open. "Let's go downtown somewhere for dinner."

Callie decided quickly. "Yes."

The car was a new black Lincoln sedan. Clayton drove carefully, taking Park Avenue down out of Harlem.

Callie asked him why the club was closed.

Clayton was offhand with his answer. "We're going to do some renovation. The place hasn't had any work done on it for several years. It shouldn't take more than a few weeks or so."

In midtown Clayton left the car in a parking garage. They went to Elie's, an expensive French restaurant near Fifth Avenue in the sixties. Clayton ordered Dom Perignon champagne and then picked the dinner courses. Callie observed that the manager and the waiters knew Clayton as a regular customer.

Clayton asked her about herself. She and Holland had previously prepared a cover story to tell Clayton when the time came, mixing truth and fiction.

She told him that she had been born and raised in Forest Hills, had graduated from Queens College, and lived at home in Forest Hills with her father, a brother, and a sister. Truth. That she worked as an editor for a small technical publisher on Sixth Avenue, editing computer handbooks. Fiction. Holland had arranged with the publishing company, which did small printing jobs for the police department from time to time, to back up Callie's story if there were any inquiries about her.

Clayton, in turn, told her what she guessed was also a mixture of truth and fiction. He said he'd been born in New York City but after his parents started living apart they'd sent him when he was still a small boy to stay with relatives in Ireland. He'd spent most of his youth in schools in Ireland, London, and Switzerland.

Callie had noticed that when he ordered dinner he'd spoken excellent French and now she knew why.

He said that over the years he'd returned from time to time for visits in New York but that after he finished college in London, he'd managed and was a partner in a bar there and later a restaurant.

"About six months ago my relatives in Ireland told me about a distant cousin of ours here in New York, Terrence McCord, who needed help. He was ill, his wife had died, and he wanted someone in the family to come and be with him. It wasn't a money problem, I was told. He was well-off. The family urged me to try to help him, so I sold my interest in my business and came here."

Clayton took a sip of champagne and said that for the past several months he'd lived with Terrence McCord in Mc-Cord's house on Staten Island and had tried to look after his cousin's business interests which included a small trucking company on Staten Island and the Easy Street Club in Harlem.

"Then, just recently, old Terrence McCord died in his sleep." Clayton said. "And I found that I'd inherited the house, the trucking company, and the club in Harlem."

A likely story, Callie thought. What she said was, "Sounds like you've led an interesting life."

When they'd finished dinner, Clayton said he'd like to drive her home. Callie shook her head. "I always go home from the city by subway. My father or my brother always meet me when I get off the subway. I have to call home before I leave the restaurant to tell them I'm on the way."

"But I can drive you."

"No," Callie said flatly. "I don't think that would be a good idea. My family, well, they're sort of protective of me. I don't know how they'd react if you and I drove up to the house together, and I hadn't told them anything about you before."

Clayton looked at her as if he were bemused. "You mean they might not approve because of me? Don't tell me it's because of the difference between—our shades of skin."

Callie had to smile. "I like the way you put it. But yes. At least until I said something beforehand."

"But I want to see you again."

"I'll have to think about it," she said. She didn't want him to get suspicious, that she might be too eager to see him again. "Tell you what"—she wrote down the phone number of the technical publishing company and gave it to him—

"later in the week if you still want to see me, call me. I'll let you know then."

They left the restaurant after she'd called her father and told him she was on the way home. Clayton walked her to the nearest subway station and waited with her until her train came in. He kissed her on the cheek as she stepped aboard the subway.

Hooked, Callie thought, and hoped she was right.

15

Anne looked slowly around the room where the members of the secret grand jury convened to hear evidence against Roy Clayton were assembled. The room was medium-size and mostly bare except for the narrow wood desks curving around in three ascending semicircles much like, Anne always thought, paintings she had seen of nineteenth-century operating theaters. The jurors sat in swivel chairs behind the desks and the foreman and the secretary sat in the top-most semicircle.

All grand juries are made up of not less than sixteen or more than twenty-three people. Today there were nineteen members present. Earlier, after this grand jury had been empaneled, the court had appointed Esther Primis foreman. The other jurors had then appointed Kevin Greenlee secretary. It was the job of Foreman Primis to swear in each witness and the duty of Secretary Greenlee to keep the records of the proceedings. The finding of an indictment would require the agreement of at least twelve of the jurors hearing the evidence.

Anne opened her address with a statement that the jurors were being charged with the duty of determining at some point whether or not an indictment should be issued in the matter of the disappearance of five men connected to organized crime groups in the New York area and the shooting death of a sixth man.

"Today," she told the jurors, "you will hear certain testimony indicating circumstantial evidence of a link between these events and one individual, Roy Clayton, about whom you will learn more as we proceed."

Anne stepped aside and John Holland was sworn in by Esther Primis. Holland gave a concise summary of the activities of Terrence McCord while he was alive, stressing that for about a quarter of a century McCord had run the biggest burglary ring in New York City, with the cooperation and approval of the area's five organized crime families. Holland passed around photographs of certain members of those crime families.

"Look at them carefully," he instructed, and explained that next the jurors were going to see a videotape made by his organized Crime Task Force at the funeral of Terrence McCord. Then he ran the tape, pointing out the organized crime family members who had attended and, for the first time, showing them Roy Clayton on the film shot at the cemetery that day.

The videotape ended and Holland was replaced by the next witness for the district attorney: Fred Reeves, of the police Intelligence Unit. Reeves testified that on July 12 a court-approved listening device installed in Salvatora's Café had picked up the conversation the jurors were about to hear. He then played the tape recording of the discussion between Carmine Lutos and someone Reeves called Bo-Bo revealing the contract that was out for a hit on Roy Clayton.

"We've got arrest warrants out on both of the individuals you just heard," Reeves told the jurors. "If you're wondering why we don't have a last name for the person on the tape I identified as "Bo-Bo," it's because we don't have a last name for him yet. The business these guys are in, they appear out of nowhere, do a job here or there, and often as not move on."

Holland returned as a witness to continue giving evidence. "After we were notified by the Intelligence Unit of the existence of the tape you have just heard, I went to the Easy Street Club in Harlem known to be frequented by Roy Clayton. Following departmental policy I informed Clayton we had information that his life might be in danger. He appeared to brush off the news. The events you will hear about next occurred starting on the same night after I had spoken to Roy Clayton."

Police officer J. J. Hoffer followed Holland as a witness. He described how he and his partner had found a deserted Cadillac on the West Side Highway, windows shot out, the front seat covered in blood. He explained that a check with motor vehicle registration showed that the Cadillac belonged to a Joey Rocco. The jurors were shown photographs of the car at the time it was found.

In rapid succession the jurors next heard testimony about the discovery of the Buick belonging to Albert Turno, the abduction of Louis Ugo from his house in Brooklyn Heights, the abduction of Dino Capri in Hoboken, and the abduction of Nicholas Dolayga and the shooting of the bodyguard, Bobby Divers, in Salvatora's Café.

Anne then made a final address to the jurors. "In the days, and if necessary weeks, to come we will return to you in subsequent proceedings to offer continuing information in this case as it develops. Thank you for your attention and your service here today."

Anne stepped back, gathered up her notes, stuffed them into her attaché case, and left the room. Downstairs in the building Holland caught up with her and said, "Good show, Annie."

She agreed. "I think it went well. You were fine, all the witnesses were, I could see that the jurors had no trouble following the connection we were trying to make in the case. I think we were right not to present Callie at this time."

Holland nodded.

They had decided, after Callie had reported her account of the night she had had dinner with Roy Clayton, to reserve her testimony until a later time, especially since she might be seeing Clayton again.

Holland had turned his beeper off while he was in the grand jury room. He turned it back on and saw that he had received a call. The phone number was unfamiliar to him but he recognized the area code preceding the number was for Queens.

"I'd better check this call out," Holland said. "See you tonight?"

Anne winked. "You'd better."

He watched her walk away until she was out of sight. He went to the phone booth on the corner and dialed the number showing on his beeper.

A man's voice answered, "Can I help you?"

"This is Lieutenant John Holland."

"Lieutenant, I'm Sergeant Jessup, Homicide, Queens. I'm calling you about an NYPD detective, Henry Grisham. I checked with NYPD headquarters. They said Grisham was in your command."

"Yeah. What about him?"

"Well, you see, Lieutenant, we just found his body—"

"Found it where? What happened to him?"

"Shot. Looks like a self-inflicted wound. We're here at his apartment now. I thought you'd want to know."

"I'll be right there," Holland said.

"You know where his apartment is?"

"I know," Holland said. "Astoria. I'm on my way."

Sergeant Neal Jessup met Holland at the door of Henry Grisham's studio apartment. From the hallway Holland could see other men moving around inside the room. Before Holland went inside, Sergeant Jessup said, "We've been here for about an hour. We got a call from the building super here, saying a man had been shot. We came right away."

Holland could see that Jessup was sizing him up with wary eyes. Probably because of the difference in their ranks, Holland thought. The sergeant was young, his face still boyish-looking, his brownish hair parted in a straight line on the left side of his head and plastered down by some kind of stickum tonic. Holland wanted to put him at ease.

"I really appreciate the call," Holland said. "I wanted to be here strictly on a personal basis. Grisham was one of my best men. I'll stay out of your way."

"Sure," Jessup said, moving ahead into the apartment. "The super lives in a basement apartment right beneath here. He says he heard a noise, at first he thought it was a car backfiring, but it sounded like it came from here. He says he hadn't seen Grisham around for a few days and he decided to come up and check the apartment. Nobody answered when he knocked on the door so he used his key. He found the body just the way you see it."

Holland walked over and looked down at the body. Grisham was lying on the floor, his head and shoulders part-way under an armchair. The gun, a .38 revolver, was in his right hand, the barrel of the gun thrust into his mouth. There was a dark pool of blood spread out on the bare floor under the back of his head.

The body was fully clothed, checkered shirt, khaki jacket, dark slacks, socks, and shoes. On a small round table next to the armchair was an almost empty bottle of scotch and a glass with about an inch of scotch still in it.

"We didn't want to move the body until you saw it," Jessup said. "The M.E.'s already been here. He estimated the time of death as within an hour before we got here, which would fit it as soon before the super called it in."

Holland looked around the room. There was the arm-chair, the small round table, a sleep sofa, and a chest of drawers. The night he had taken Henry Grisham to dinner and brought him home, Holland had not come into the apartment. He felt a profound sadness now that Grisham had lived in such bleak surroundings these last months which, as it had turned out, were to be the final days of his life.

Holland said to the sergeant, "I'd like it if you'd notify me when the medical examiner releases the body. I'll take care of the burial arrangements."

"Yes, sir, Lieutenant." They shook hands.

Holland dreaded what he had to do next: notify Anne that Grisham had committed suicide.

16

Anne was weary when Matt Slater dropped her off in front of her house that evening and drove away. In an hour Holland would be there. When he'd called her in the afternoon she would have suggested that they cancel their date, except that he told her Henry Grisham had committed suicide. She knew they had to talk.

She walked to the front door of the house and a figure stepped out of the shadows and confronted her. She thought, God! I'm about to be mugged!

"D.A. Gilman, it's me. Sergeant Cody, Internal Affairs. Did I startle you?"

She looked at Cody, grim-faced. "Yeah, you sure as hell did! What are you doing lurking around here?" Her momentary fear had made her angry.

"Look, I'm sorry," Cody said. "I needed to talk to you."

"Then why didn't you come to my office? I don't appreciate anyone coming unannounced to my home."

Cody was shifting from foot to foot. "I understand. I really do. And I'd never think of bothering you in this fashion if it wasn't important."

Anne said, "All right, get on with it. What did you want to see me about that was so important?"

"Did you hear what happened to Detective Grisham? You know, on the Organized Crime Task Force, I told you about, might be passing information to Roy Clayton."

Anne decided not to answer directly. "What about him?"

"I heard it this afternoon. They say he committed suicide."

"I still think that's something you could have told me about at the office," Anne said.

All at once, out of nowhere except instinct, she was getting bad vibes about this conversation. What was Cody doing here at her house, telling her all this? Fleetingly, knowing it could be momentary paranoia, she thought, He might be wearing a wire.

Cody was shaking his head. "No. no. It's too risky for me to be seen talking to you."

"Too risky for whom?"

"Me! Me!"

Anne put out a hand as if to push him back. "Sergeant, I have no idea what you're talking about. Say what you have to say. And say it now."

"I'm thinking maybe somebody's trying to cover up for Grisham," Cody said, his voice a whisper. "Bury the whole business, that he was a rogue cop."

"Who? Who would want to do that?"

"It's happened before. Guys in the department who don't want a big scandal breaking," Cody said.

"That's a very serious allegation, Sergeant. Do you have any proof to back it up?"

"Well," he said, "it seems to me something's not kosher that right after I suspect Grisham's maybe in the pay of Roy Clayton, Grisham ups and commits suicide. I'm wondering what kind of investigation you might have begun after I told you what I suspected about him, who else might have known from you of my suspicions. And maybe figured it was time Grisham was removed from the picture."

Anne was astonished. "Are you actually suggesting he didn't commit suicide?"

"I'm suggesting it's a possibility, yeah. And if somebody did get rid of him they might want to get rid of me next. That's why I wondered who you might have told what I told you."

"This conversation's gone far enough, Sergeant Cody," Anne said. "When the district attorney's office is ready to inform you of any investigation, formal or informal, undertaken with regard to your suspicions about Detective Grisham, you will be informed. Until then you will communicate with me only through official channels. Good-night, Sergeant."

Anne went into the house, watching Russell Cody cross the street, get into a red Honda parked there, and drive away. She locked the door. She was shaken by the encounter with Cody. By now, she thought, Holland should be home. It would be better if she met him at his apartment instead of having him come to her house. Cody could return and be lurking around somewhere watching what she did next. She decided to phone Holland before she bathed and dressed and went to meet him.

Holland made a pitcher of martinis and put the pitcher in the refrigerator for Anne when she got to the apartment. He fixed himself a Jack Daniel's and water and stood at the window looking out to the southeast at the lighted windows of the United Nations building catercorner across First Avenue from his apartment, the dark East River behind the UN, and the curving line of lights of Queens on the far side of the river.

Holland's corner apartment was on the seventeenth floor of the Tudor City complex of buildings on Forty-second

Street and First Avenue. When the buildings had gone co-op a few years earlier Holland had bought a one-bedroom apartment. The place suited him fine. It was centrally located, had a view, and with a large living room, bedroom, kitchen, and bath, made a comfortable bachelor pad.

He could tell from the sound of Anne's voice on the phone when she'd called him that something had happened that had upset her, although all she had said was, "John, I don't want to talk now. But I'm coming over to your place. Wait for me. I'll be there within the hour."

He finished his drink, made himself another one, and the intercom rang from the lobby. The doorman announced that Anne was on her way up. Holland stood in the open doorway until she got off the elevator and came walking quickly into the apartment. After he'd shut and locked the door he handed her the martini he'd prepared.

"Now sit," he said. "It's my turn to serve you. I have a feeling you might need this."

She nodded and drank some of the martini.

Holland said, "All right, what's wrong? Tell me."

Anne took another sip of martini. "That detective. From Internal Affairs. Sergeant Cody. He was at my house waiting for me when I got home tonight. I was furious that he was there. I told him it was improper. He gave me a lot of double-talk about the reason he was there was because of the death of Detective Grisham. He said maybe it wasn't suicide, maybe it was murder, a cover-up."

"Murder? A cover-up?" Holland was shaking his head. "I don't believe this guy! He must be out of his skull."

"That's not all. He was asking me a lot of—tricky questions. I think he could have been wearing a wire."

"Hey! Hey! Hey!" Holland said. "Hold on. Go back, tell me exactly what he said, what you said."

She told him the conversation she'd had with Cody.

"While we were talking," she added, "suddenly I had this eerie feeling he was taping everything we were saying. I thought I picked up that he was asking me a lot of leading questions."

Holland glanced at her. "I don't know why he'd be taping you. For what purpose? But in any event, from what you've told me you said, I can't see where it would do him any good."

"I'm not exactly worried about what I said today, even if he was taping me."

"Then what?"

"Don't you see," Anne said slowly, "if Cody is convinced Detective Grisham was passing on information to Roy Clayton, now he's convinced somebody killed Grisham to cover it up before there could be an investigation of the charge. And that possibly I—or somebody—was in on the cover-up. That's what I think Cody is trying to prove."

"But there was no cover-up," Holland said.

"Maybe not. The fact remains, however, that I didn't do anything with the information Cody brought me about Grisham."

Holland said, "Because I asked you not to until I had a chance to talk to Grisham—"

"I know that and you know that," Anne said. "But—well, what if it turns out Detective Grisham didn't commit suicide? That he was killed by someone?"

Holland finished his drink before he answered.

"Let's consider this situation carefully, see if we can put it into some kind of perspective that makes sense. First of all, out of nowhere Sergeant Cody accosts you outside your office and tells you that he thinks Hank Grisham is passing departmental information to Roy Clayton, right?"

"Yes."

"But Cody can't give you any solid proof, just his suspicions."

"Yes, that's right."

"Now," Holland said, "everything indicated Grisham committed suicide, but, again, Cody appears suggesting Grisham could have been murdered as part of a cover-up. But, again, he has no proof to offer. That's the situation, isn't it?"

Anne nodded. "That's the situation."

Holland leaned toward her. "Let me tell you a story about this guy I knew a few years back in the department. His name was Toby something, Toby Ellers, as I remember. He was an electronics expert, did all the wiretapping for the Intelligence Unit. After several years on the job he began to act peculiar. He got this idea somebody was tailing him and then that all *his* conversations were being tapped and taped. It got so he wouldn't talk to anyone. He'd communicate by writing on a piece of paper whatever he wanted to say and then after he'd shown it to you he'd tear the paper up. Finally, he stopped coming into work. He'd gotten so that he wouldn't leave his house, wouldn't go outside, had his telephone disconnected. In the end he was retired on disability from the department and the last I heard he was in a mental hospital, totally freaked out, completely paranoid. He'd succumbed to suggestibility; a hypochondriac of the psyche was the way one of the shrinks put it."

"You think that's what's happening with Russell Cody?" Anne asked. "You think I'm in danger of becoming a bit paranoid myself?"

"As far as Cody's concerned," Holland said, "I would guess that some people can't have a job like he has, always looking for conspiracies, without suspecting that conspiracies exist even when there's no proof. Today in police work, where we're tapping the criminals, and maybe they're tapping us, for all I know, and we plant undercover agents among them and they manage to turn a detective here and there to feed them information, it's not all that different from what went on between our CIA and the Russians' KGB during the Cold War. Except that now we all have more advanced methods in eavesdropping, computer tracking, the ability to conduct surveillance from a distance, to invade the innermost privacy of one another."

Anne smiled slightly. "Which means, if you stop to think about it, that a bit of paranoia now and then is inevitable, is that what you're saying?"

"Even more than that, I'd say we'd all have to be a little crazy not to be a bit paranoid now and then, considering the technological fishbowl we live in today."

"Whew!" Anne said. "I don't think I want to think about it."

Holland laughed. "I don't think I've really told you anything you didn't already know, anything that most of us didn't already know. You probably just haven't heard it articulated this way before."

Anne held out her empty glass. "On that note, I think I'll have another martini."

"Good idea."

Holland went to the refrigerator, filled her glass from the pitcher, when his telephone rang. He handed Anne the martini as he picked up the phone. She saw him frowning as he listened to the phone, then he hung up and turned toward her. He said, "That was the dispatcher calling. A report came in that there's been some kind of an explosion, fire, at the Easy Street Club, Clayton's place."

"Let's go," Anne said, already standing. "My car's parked right downstairs."

17

They saw the flames and smoke of the fire while they were still several blocks away. There were seven fire engines up ahead and a dozen police cars clearly visible, along with the flames and smoke, in the illumination of the floodlights that had been set up in the street. There were crowds of people from the area watching from the sidewalks, and the block where the fire was raging had been cordoned off by the police.

Anne left the car parked at the curb and followed Holland up to the wooden barricades set up by the police. Holland showed his shield to one of the patrolmen on duty and he let them through, pointing out in answer to Holland's question the police sergeant from the nearby Harlem precinct who was in charge at the scene.

Holland and Anne approached the sergeant, Holland again identifying them both. "This could involve one of my cases," he explained to the sergeant. "You have any information on who or what caused the fire?"

The sergeant, whose hands, face, and neck were

smudged with soot, said, "There were some witnesses out on the street who saw what happened. According to their statements a small black van pulled up in front of the building about an hour ago. Four or five men jumped out of the back of the van and tossed several Molotov cocktails through the plate glass door and window of the club. The whole building went up as if a bomb had been set off inside. The guys jumped back into the van and it took off."

"Anybody get a description of the van, the guys?" Holland asked.

"Not enough to do us any good. We already radioed in an APB to be on the lookout for the van," the sergeant said. "There is one other thing. Witnesses who are familiar with the club say that just before the van got there the bartender who works at the club came out the front door and walked up the block to his car. Then the place was firebombed. They say that when the van sped away, the bartender in his car took off after it. Hard to say whether he was in on what happened or was chasing after them. That's about all we know."

Holland nodded. "Thanks a lot, Sergeant."

Holland and Anne walked back out of the way and stood watching the raging fire. Dozens of firemen were trying to put out the flames with water and foam. Several television news teams had arrived and were filming scenes of the burning building.

Anne said, "Thank God the club had been closed up. Otherwise, Callie Brinnin might have come here and been inside."

Holland agreed. "I guess Clayton suspected something like this might happen. That's probably why he closed the place up."

The sergeant Holland had questioned came hurrying toward them, saying, "Lieutenant, we just heard over the police radio there's been a big shoot-out down near Chinatown involving a van that fits the description of the one seen here." He gave Holland the location where the reported shoot-out had occurred.

Anne said, "Looks like the missing van has turned up, all right."

"I think you can count on that," Holland agreed.

They were standing, again inside an area marked off by police—this time with yellow tape reading CRIME SCENE DO NOT ENTER—a few feet away from a black van with its rear door flung open revealing the blood-splattered interior. The van had run up onto the sidewalk and smashed into a fire hydrant.

There were police, in uniforms and in plain clothes, standing in a group inside the sealed off area. An Emergency Service truck was parked at the corner and there were squad cars and two EMS ambulances on the side of the street opposite the van.

Anne knew one of the plainclothes detectives who had been inspecting the interior of the van. He was Captain Edwin Jeffers of the Manhattan South Precinct.

Jeffers seemed surprised when he turned away from the van and recognized Anne as she and Holland walked toward him. When Anne was an assistant D.A. she and Jeffers had worked on a couple of cases together. The captain looked at Anne quizzically. "What brings you here, District Attorney Gilman?"

Anne introduced Holland, then said, "We think whatever happened here may be connected with a case under current investigation."

Jeffers rubbed a hand across his face. "I sure as hell hope it's connected to something because we don't have much to go on so far. Apparently there was a wild shoot-out here. According to the witnesses we've managed to locate, five or six men in this van were shot—"

"And the bodies?" Anne asked. "Have they been taken to the morgue?"

"None of the bodies were left behind after the shooting." Jeffers shook his head. "The witnesses we've talked to say that whoever was responsible for this took the bodies away with them. It doesn't make sense."

"Were there many witnesses to everything that happened?" Holland asked.

Jeffers pointed at the tenement buildings along the street where people were leaning out of windows watching the action below. "A hot night like tonight you always have people trying to get cool by sitting by their open windows. The people who have been willing to talk to us agree on what they saw. They say the van drove up and parked in front of that bar." Jeffers motioned toward a small dimly lit bar midway in the block. "They say five, maybe six, men emerged from the van and went into the bar. About a half hour later the men came out and got into the van again, a couple of them sitting in the front, the others in the rear. The van started up and pulled away from the curb and that's when it happened."

The captain looked up the block and continued, "At that point a large truck came around the corner, rammed into the van, and sent it crashing into the fire hydrant. At the same time there was an explosion of gunfire from the truck ripping into the van. There were so many bullets that the back panel of the truck looks like a sieve. There were a few brief shots fired in return from the van and then the shooting stopped. When it did, according to the witnesses, men jumped from the truck, pulled all the bodies out of the van, and flung the bodies, one after another, into the open rear door of the truck. The men from the truck then jumped back inside, slammed the rear door, and the truck roared away."

Anne asked, "Did you get any description of the gunmen, the truck?"

Jeffers looked around at the people still watching from the windows in the surrounding buildings. "Only what you'd expect, given the circumstances. You know how it goes in a

126

situation like this; nothing detailed enough to do us much good."

The captain paused before he said, "I've been wondering. It just occurred to me. This shoot-out, the way the bodies were whisked away afterward. I know about those other recent cases where the same kind of thing happened. Is there a connection? Do you think there's a connection?"

"That's what we hope to find out," Anne said. "Sooner or later."

"I'll let you know anything I find," Jeffers said.

Anne and then Holland shook hands with Jeffers, Anne saying, "I know you will, Captain. And I'll do the same with you."

Anne and Holland went back to her car and drove uptown. "Lay it out for me the way you see it," she said to Holland. "Let's see if we agree."

"It's almost surely Roy Clayton's handiwork. The bartender up at the Easy Street Club followed the van down here. He watched the men go into the bar, then called Clayton and told him what had happened and where the men were. Clayton dispatched a crew here and exacted his swift revenge for the firebombing of his place and, to announce that it was his doing, followed the pattern of his earlier executions by taking the bodies away. Which makes—what?— ten, maybe eleven, bodies gone, just like that."

"You know," Anne said, "if Clayton's behind all this and he's found a way to dispose of the bodies where they'll never be found, this case will be the hardest gangland series of slayings to crack since the time of Murder, Incorporated. Here the problem is if we can't find the bodies how are we going to make a connection with who's guilty. Back then the problem was that hit men from out of town who had no connection with the intended victims were imported to do the killings and then left town. That case might never have been solved without an informer."

"Let's hope we have better luck," Holland said.

18

Charley Stenten walked into Frank Cavenaugh's office on the third floor of the 16th Precinct at 8:45 A.M. Cavenaugh had phoned Stenten at his apartment three quarters of an hour earlier.

"We just picked up the son of a bitch Peter Holmer," Cavenaugh had said. "We'll be interrogating him in about an hour. I thought you might want to be here."

Stenten had said that yeah, he would be there. He called his office and left a message where he would be. He took a cab instead of the subway—it was already unbearably hot. He left his tie and jacket off until he reached the precinct.

Cavenaugh was talking on the phone and waved Stenten to a chair. Stenten put on his tie and jacket while he waited for Cavenaugh to finish his phone conversation.

When Cavenaugh hung up, he said, "You made good time, Charley. Let's go down and see what we can dredge out of this guy."

As they rode the elevator to the first floor and walked to the interrogation room at the rear of the building, Cave-

"I already told you my name; Peter Holmer, remember?"

"I told you I have nothing to say to you."

"Hang on! You'd better listen, lady! I told you what I wanted! You'd better see that I get it! You meet me Sunday. You know where. And you'd better have the money or I'm going to tell the police everything I know about your husband's murder!"

Cruz turned off the tape recorder.

Cavenaugh said, "Does that answer your question, Holmer? Let's start over again. You want to tell us what you know about the deaths of Richard Krager and Kenneth Shuba? We've already got enough on tape to send you away on a charge of extortion. You tell us something that'll help us sort out the deaths of Krager and Shuba, well, we'll take into account that you were trying to assist us."

Holmer made a gesture with his finger. "You ask me do I want to tell you what I know about their deaths, I'll tell you what I want; I want a lawyer."

"You were already read your rights. You said you didn't need a lawyer," Cavenaugh said.

"That was before I found out you're trying to frame me on some phony charge. I want a lawyer. I'm not answering any questions. I'm not talking to you anymore until I get a lawyer."

"Okay, have it your way," Cavenaugh said. "Later you may wish you'd talked now." Cavenaugh nodded to Cruz. "Take him away. See that he gets a lawyer. Lock him up meanwhile."

Stenten and Cavenaugh left the interrogation room.

"He'll talk," Cavenaugh said. "Soon as he gets a lawyer and we play that tape, the lawyer'll advise him to make a deal."

"What about the girl, Bonnie what's her name?" Stenten asked.

"Bonnie Seywood. Hell, I doubt that she knows anything. Holmer's the one who can tell us what we want to know."

"You mind if I talk to her while you still have her here?" Stenten asked.

"Be my guest," Cavenaugh said indifferently. "Come on, I'll take you to her."

They walked through the first floor of the precinct to a series of holding cells down a corridor behind the booking desk. On the way Cavenaugh picked up a transcript of the interview he'd had with Bonnie Seywood earlier and gave it to Stenten.

When they reached the series of seven holding cells, all the cells were empty except for one where Bonnie Seywood sat on the bottom mattress of a bunk bed. The cell door was unlocked and Cavenaugh swung the door open and said, "Bonnie, this is Lieutenant Stenten. He wants to talk to you."

"Then can I go?" she asked.

"We'll decide after you've talked to him," Cavenaugh answered.

Cavenaugh left Stenten in the cell after Stenten said he'd check with him before leaving the precinct. Stenten sat on a small stool facing her.

According to the transcript of the interview Cavenaugh had had with her she'd said she was twenty-four years old. But she was, Stenten thought as he looked at her, one of those waiflike child-women who could be any age, small in size, a plain face, a body that could just as easily be a boy's body, black hair cut so short that it looked like a skullcap. She had on a blue halter dress and scuffed loafers.

She sat far back on the bunk bed with her arms crossed over her chest.

"I don't want you to be frightened, Bonnie," Stenten said. "Let me explain to you that I work for the district attorney. As you've been told we're investigating the deaths of Richard Krager and Kenneth Shuba. You worked in the video store with Kenneth Shuba, I believe?"

"Yes," she whispered.

"Yes." Stenten smiled. "And you and Peter Holmer are friends?"

"Yes."

"Peter's your boyfriend, I bet."

She nodded. "Sort of."

"And this morning when you went to his apartment and took a suitcase to him you just wanted to help him because he's sort of your boyfriend?"

"I didn't know I was going to get into any trouble for just doing that."

"Of course you didn't." Stenten moved his stool a little closer to her. "And you're not in any trouble yet. But there are some facts you have to understand. I want you to listen to me closely, and if you have any questions, I want you to ask me, okay?"

"Okay."

"Bonnie, I want you to realize that Peter Holmer's in trouble, serious trouble, and he's going to jail even if we don't find out anything more from him or you than we know now. And there's nothing you can do to help him or hurt him. That's the truth and I want you to believe me."

"Okay, I believe you."

Stenten said, "However, we're at a point now where it's you who can be hurt or helped, you who can be in serious trouble and can go to jail, unless you tell me the truth about questions I'm going to ask you."

She looked like she was going to cry. "What—do you want to know?"

"Peter and Kenneth Shuba lived in the same building. Were they friends?"

"Yes. That's how I met Peter. He and Ken were friends and Peter used to come to the store and Ken introduced us and then I started going around with Peter."

"Did you know," Stenten asked, "that after Richard Krager and Kenneth Shuba were shot to death in Krager's apartment, Peter threatened Richard Krager's wife, Bettina Krager? That Peter told her he was going to the police and tell them the truth about the two killings unless she paid him to keep quiet? Did you know that?"

Bonnie looked at Stenten and wiped tears from her eyes.

Stenten said quickly, "The police taped a telephone conversation where Peter threatened Mrs. Krager. We already have that. The tape we have is enough to send Peter to jail. What I want to know from you, and if you don't tell me the truth, you could go to jail too, is: Did you know about what Peter was doing?"

"Not exactly."

"What does that mean, not exactly?"

The tears were rolling down her cheeks. "He—he'll *kill* me if I say anything else—"

"He won't kill you," Stenten said flatly. "I guarantee you. Now, did you know what Peter was doing?"

"I knew he was doing something but he didn't exactly tell me. I guessed for myself. See, before that night I knew Ken was going to the Krager apartment. Peter told me Ken told him that he was going to rob the apartment, only it wouldn't be a real robbery—"

"Wouldn't be a real robbery? How do you mean?"

She fluttered her hand in the air. "What Peter said was that Ken told him Mr. Krager *asked* him to rob the apartment, take some stuff, and Mr. Krager would collect insurance—"

Stenten said, "Wait a minute! Are you saying Shuba knew Richard Krager?"

"Oh sure. I even knew Mr. Krager. He used to come to the store to see Ken."

"How would they know one another, Shuba and Krager?"

"Like I said, Mr. Krager used to come to the store. I wasn't supposed to know what they were talking about. But I did. For the longest time Ken wanted to make his own movies. You know, the kind, where people—you know, make out."

"Pornographic movies you mean?"

"Yeah." She nodded her head. "I couldn't think of what they call them."

"So," Stenten said, "Shuba wanted to make these movies—what did that have to do with Krager?"

"He told Ken he'd give him the money. Only later, when the time came, Mr. Krager said he didn't have the money and that's when he told Ken if there was a robbery at his apartment he could say a whole lot of valuable things were taken and he'd collect the insurance and then he'd be able to give Ken enough to make his movies."

"And Shuba agreed to the robbery, is that what you're saying?"

She shook her head back and forth. "No. No. Before that night Ken told Peter there'd been a change in plans. He didn't tell Peter what the change was. All he would say was that he was going to do something bigger than a robbery and he was going to get—I think he told Peter—a hundred thousand dollars for what he was going to do."

Stenten frowned, thinking. "Did Shuba, Ken, ever tell Peter how he was going to get into the apartment? Whether to rob it or whatever other thing he was going to do?"

"Yeah. He told Peter that he'd been to the apartment to see Mr. Krager several times. And that Mr. Krager had given him keys to the door of the building and to the apartment and had told him the doorman who would be there at the time he should come usually took a break and wasn't watching around that time."

"And then," Stenten prompted, "there was the night that both Kenneth Shuba and Richard Krager were shot, so the question is: How did Peter think he could get any money out of Mrs. Krager by threatening her that he'd tell the police the truth about what happened? Did Peter ever explain that to you?"

"Sort of." She thought for a moment. "See, Peter was always talking about this and that. Sometimes I'd listen, sometimes I wouldn't pay any attention. You know? Anyhow, from what he said, he'd figured all along that maybe this something Ken was going to do, and wouldn't exactly tell him, was kill somebody. Only when Ken and Mr. Krager both got shot and killed, Peter decided that maybe it was Mrs. Krager who somewhere met Ken and that she was the one who told him she'd pay him to kill her husband. And that that's what Ken did that night and then Mrs. Krager shot and killed Ken. Peter talked about how he was going to get the money that should have gone to Ken from her. Peter was always dreaming up stuff like that."

Stenten took a deep breath. "We know Peter tried to get the money from Mrs. Krager and she wouldn't pay him. Did he ever tell you anything about that?"

"No. Never. I didn't know anything about that, honest. And I didn't know the police were looking for Peter. He suddenly showed up at my apartment and said some people were after him for money he owed them and he didn't want to go home for a few days. Then he asked me this morning to go to his apartment and pack a suitcase with some of his clothes and bring the suitcase to him. That's—what happened."

Stenten touched her arm. "You did fine, Bonnie. There's one more thing you have to do and then you can go home, okay?"

"Yes."

"I want you to tell Lieutenant Cavenaugh, the detective who questioned you earlier, everything you've told me. He'll have your statement, what you tell him, typed up and after you sign it you'll be free to leave. Will you do that?"

"I'll do it."

"Good girl," Stenten said.

19

The phone call from Arthur Hillyard in the middle of the afternoon had come at a particularly bad time for Anne.

There were nights when an inexplicable rash of crimes occurred all over the city, all requiring that an assistant D.A. be assigned to oversee the investigations. And the night before his phone call had been one of those: Three small children had been killed in a senseless drive-by shooting on the Upper West Side; the torso of an unidentified female had been found in a garbage bag lying at a curb in midtown; another fatal shooting had occurred in the subway; three stabbings had taken place in Chinatown and the three victims were not expected to live; there had been three rapes, two on a rooftop, one in a stairwell, all in Chelsea and apparently all the work of the same individual; and in Greenwich Village two senior citizens had been brutally beaten in separate push-in robberies. And Anne had been busy matching assistant D.A.s to the various cases.

Hillyard had phoned to say that it was important that he see her and asked if she could come to his office that same day. She had told him if it was that important she'd be there as soon as she could after six P.M. He had said he'd wait for her.

Hillyard's office was on a floor near the top of the World Trade Center at the tip of Manhattan. Anne arranged with Matt Slater to drive her there and to wait until her meeting ended. It was closer to seven when she walked into the lobby of the World Trade Center and stepped into the express elevator.

There was no one else on the elevator and as it shot upward she experienced a rush of adrenaline and anxiety. All her life she had experienced mild claustrophobia when she was confined in a closed space even for a brief time, and she breathed a sigh of relief when she stepped off the elevator into the spacious reception area of Hillyard's suite of offices. The floors there were plushly carpeted, music played soothingly, there were fresh-cut flowers in crystal vases, and through floor-to-ceiling windows was a sweeping vista of almost the whole of Manhattan, the Hudson River, miles of New Jersey, the Statue of Liberty, and, far out, the Atlantic Ocean.

As soon as Anne stepped off the elevator the receptionist, who recognized her, called Hillyard and he came out of his office, greeted her, kissed her on the cheek, and led her back past a dozen or so secretaries into his office. This, too, was impressive, with its thick carpeting, flowers, and panoramic view.

"I do thank you for coming, my dear," Hillyard said. "I'm not unaware of how busy you are but I thought it was most important that we talk as soon as possible."

"I assumed it was important, Arthur. Not that I wouldn't have wanted to see you any time you called."

Hillyard smiled and they talked briefly, generally about some of the cases she was handling; Anne knew he was trying to put her at ease before he brought up the subject he thought was urgent enough to have requested her to come to his office that day.

Finally, he said, "Anne dear, as I expect you know, among the contacts I have, the people I see on various levels in this city, I frequently acquire information that isn't—well, known by many other individuals. Sometimes it's confidential information that later becomes public information. Sometimes it's information about a matter or matters that later turn out to be of no consequence and are never heard of again."

He looked at her shrewdly. "I expect you already know that."

"Yes, I do know, Arthur."

"So, it is with that understanding that I tell you now what I felt you should know."

Anne nodded.

Hillyard leaned his elbow on the desk, resting his neck in the palm of his hand. "What I have heard concerning you is there is a suggestion somewhere, in some quarter, that you may have—perhaps inadvertently—been, ah, delinquent in following up evidence that was presented to you as district attorney. Evidence of a possible felony crime, and further evidence that there was a possible cover-up of this felony crime after you, it is again suggested, were delinquent in investigating the original felony."

"Arthur, I just can't believe this is happening! Who— who's suggesting—all these things?"

"I don't know the primary source of this, well, allegation, I suppose," Hillyard said. "But I do know that it is rumored there exists a tape recording of a conversation between you and another person discussing the fact that you had been given information about this possible felony. Do you know anything about such a tape?"

Anne was genuinely perplexed. "A tape recording of a conversation between me and another person?"

"So I've heard." Hillyard hesitated briefly before he said,

"Anne dear, what's far more serious is that I have also learned that the federal prosecutor is interested in the allegations and is considering conducting an investigation into them."

Anne sat upright in her chair. "I know it must sound foolish to keep repeating it. But I just can't believe this is happening!"

Hillyard held up a hand. "I want you to remember now that I told you earlier some of the information I acquire about a matter or matters, such as the one we're discussing about you, turn out to be of no consequence and are never heard of again. That may very well be the case in this situation. Let's trust so."

"Good Lord, Arthur, you don't really believe there could be any truth to these allegations, do you?"

"Ah, there is one other delicate element involved in the allegations, according to what I've heard."

"Yes, what?"

"It is my understanding that the other person supposedly involved in the taped conversation with you is a ranking police officer. That the evidence of a felony brought to you as district attorney concerned a member of this ranking officer's command. And, perhaps most damning of all, that you have a secret—intimate relationship with this ranking officer." Hillyard paused and added, "A lieutenant, so I'm led to believe."

Anne said wonderingly, "If all of these stories are floating around, no wonder the federal prosecutor is interested in investigating them. But I'm telling you, Arthur, there is no dereliction of duty on my part in not following up the allegations, the slimmest of allegations, I might add, of this possible felony, nor have I any reason to believe there has been a cover-up. Nor do I see how it is possible that there exists a tape recording of any conversation between the police lieutenant, Lieutenant John Holland is his name, and me about any of these matters."

"And as to the other aspect of these rumors," Hillyard asked gently, "that you have an intimate relationship with Lieutenant Holland?"

"That," Anne said forthrightly, "is true."

"I see. I see. That that is true does complicate things, doesn't it?"

"I suppose so," Anne said. She made a decision. "John Holland and I have been together for approximately eighteen months."

"But you kept it secret?"

"Yes," Anne said. "As much out of a sense of our personal privacy as for any other reason."

"But didn't it occur to you that it might not be judicious to be in such a relationship? When you were district attorney involved in trying cases where he was presenting evidence, I mean. Certainly, if your relationship were known it could be charged that your judgment could be influenced because of the relationship. Didn't you, either of you, ever consider that possibility?"

"Look, Arthur," Anne said, "when John and I first fell in love I was an assistant D.A. We honestly didn't think too much about a possible conflict between our personal and professional lives. We did talk about the fact that John planned to leave law enforcement to take a job as head of security for the Richler Corporation. The problem is that appointment won't be made until next year. Meanwhile, I was taken by surprise by my appointment and elevation to district attorney."

"I see." Hillyard nodded. "But did it not ever occur to either of you that perhaps you should have stopped seeing each other once you became district attorney until he left his job in the police department?"

Anne looked at Hillyard and laughed. "Arthur, don't you really know that to be in love is a bitch?"

Hillyard smiled briefly. "I suppose." He frowned. "Now, I wonder: Do you have any idea who or what may be behind all this?"

"I have a suspicion, yes. But I don't think I should go into it with you at this point."

"Very well," Hillyard said. "I can understand how such a discussion might involve confidential matters concerning your office."

"Now, Arthur, I have a question for you: Does the governor know about all this?"

"Yes. He is aware."

Anne sat forward. "Is the reason you've told me about this matter today because the governor, or anyone else, is suggesting subtly that I might consider resigning or taking leave as district attorney?"

"No, no. Absolutely not," Hillyard said firmly. "To repeat what I've already repeated, none of this may prove to be of any consequence. I've told you what I've told you today because once I learned of the matter I felt you should be informed. There is nothing more to it than that."

"I thank you, Arthur."

Hillyard stood up from his desk and walked to her and put a hand on her shoulder. "I've known you all your life, Anne dear. I have the utmost confidence in your integrity. I accept everything you've told me. I'm sure that if any more comes of this matter you will be able to resolve it."

Anne said, "I believe I can, yes."

"I do want you to know, moreover, that if you need my help you have only to ask."

Anne stood. "I know that, Arthur. And it's reassuring. It means a great deal to me."

Hillyard smiled. "Good, good, then." As he walked her to the lobby, he added, "Let's have dinner soon. I mean the three of us; I'd like to meet your young man, the lieutenant. Not because of anything we discussed today. But because you've always been like my own daughter and so of course I'd like to meet the man you love."

"I think dinner would be nice," Anne said. "And I'd like John to meet you."

She kissed Hillyard on the cheek. "I'll phone you within the next few days and we'll set a date."

The elevator came. As she plummeted downward she felt that she was more closed in by bewildering events than by the physical confines of the elevator car.

20

That morning Callie Brinnin had received a message from the technical publishing company where she had told Roy Clayton she worked. The message was that Clayton had phoned, said he wanted to speak with Callie, and when told she was out of the office, had left a number asking that she call him back.

Callie recognized that the area code of the number Clayton had left was Staten Island. She phoned him in the afternoon and he said he'd like to take her to dinner that night and would pick her up at 5:30 at her office. She agreed to meet him, told him the address on Sixth Avenue, and said she would be waiting for him in front of the building. After she hung up, she found Holland and told him about Clayton's call and that he was taking her to dinner.

At 5:30 she was outside the building on Sixth Avenue when Clayton arrived, this time in a chauffeur-driven black Cadillac. Clayton stepped out of the car and held the door as he helped her inside, saying, "I thought it would be a nice surprise for you tonight to meet my mother. I thought we'd have dinner at my house so you could meet her. Is that all right with you?"

Callie *was* surprised. "I think that would be fine," she told him.

There was a bar in the back of the Cadillac and Clayton poured them each a glass of champagne as they drove through Brooklyn and across the Verrazano Bridge to Staten Island. Clayton explained that he and his mother lived in the house that Terrence McCord had owned and left to Clayton, along with the Easy Street Club in Harlem.

The drive took about forty-five minutes. When they reached the house, Callie saw that it was an impressive brick structure set behind a high white-walled enclosure with a curving driveway leading from the wrought iron front gate to the house. She noticed that there were two men in the gatehouse next to the entrance to the driveway.

Another man met them at the door. Clayton led her into the house and into a sitting room where the windows looked out over a rose garden. The room itself contained what looked to Callie like expensive furnishings, settees, love seats, a baby grand piano, Oriental rugs on the floor, tapestries and oil paintings on the wall.

"Why, what a lovely room," Callie said, looking around and, when Clayton motioned to it, taking a place on one of the love seats near a window. Clayton sat on the piano stool.

He said, "Terrence McCord loved this house. He spent a lot of time and money fixing it the way he wanted it to be, the way you see it today."

Callie smiled. "I'd say he certainly succeeded."

Clayton stood and moved a small coffee table between the love seat where Callie sat and the piano stool as a woman came into the room carrying a tray with cups and a tea service on it. The woman was chocolate-skinned, almost as dark as Callie. She had silver hair parted in the middle and combed back from her face, the features of which were finely chiseled. She wore a dark long-skirted dress with a lace collar and a small embroidered apron.

The woman put the tray on the coffee table and as she straightened up Clayton took her hand and said, "Callie, I want you to meet my mother, Salla Clayton. Mother, this is Callie Brinnin, whom you've heard about."

Callie stood, hastily and awkwardly, as Clayton's mother took her hand, saying, "I've been looking forward to meeting you, Callie Brinnin."

Callie tried to hide her shock and surprise at having first mistaken the woman who had entered the room for the maid. Callie noticed that Clayton himself was regarding her discomfort with amusement.

"Mrs. Clayton," Callie managed to say, "I'm so pleased to meet you."

"Do me a favor, Callie," Clayton's mother said. "Please call me Salla. Everyone does."

"All right."

Clayton moved to the coffee table, saying, "Mother, you sit there next to Callie. I'll pour the tea."

Clayton passed the teacups around, taking one for himself as he sat back down on the piano stool, and then laughed. "Callie, as you've probably guessed by now, the time has come for me and for Salla to tell you our story. I think you'll find it amusing when you think back to the night we had dinner and you said you'd have to prepare your family for—as I believe I put it—the difference between the shades of your skin and mine. Mother, why don't you start the story."

Salla looked at Callie and smiled softly and Callie thought what a truly stunning-looking female Salla must have been when she was younger.

Salla said, "This all goes back a long time ago. I was about nineteen years old and living in Harlem where I was born and raised. People thought I had a good voice and I sang in the church choir when I was a child, and later I decided I wanted to become a singer. At that time the Apollo Theatre was the place where every singer wanted to perform. Well, I knew you had to have experience before you ever got a chance to sing there, so, for a long time, I sang wherever I could, lots of little places."

She paused and took a sip of tea. "Those places, I don't think anyone who ever came to them cared much about listening to the singers. I thought I wasn't going to have much of a career. Then I heard about this new club that had opened, the Easy Street. It was run by a white man, Terrence McCord, I heard, and people said he was interested in singers and that customers were coming there from downtown as well as Harlem because of the talent that performed in his club. So, I finally got up my nerve and I went there and I auditioned for this Mr. Terrence McCord—and he hired me."

Clayton interrupted. "Mother, tell Callie what he said the first time he heard you sing."

"Oh well." Salla smiled. "He told me right then that someday I was going to be a big star and that I could sing in his club for as long as I wanted. You can't imagine what a thrill it was for me."

"Tell her about the people who came to hear you sing," Clayton prompted.

"Oh yes." Salla looked at Callie and smiled again. "It wasn't long after I started singing that people came from every place to hear me. It was a magical time! Duke Ellington came. Johnny Mercer—he wrote wonderful music and lyrics—was there. Some musicians who were so talented and the world has never heard of them, Lawson Vassells, Al Moritz, Ralph Gundersdorff, Jennifer Maceley, Cora Benlen. And one special night Benny Goodman came to the club and told me he was there because he'd heard of me."

Salla took a sip of tea. "Pretty soon I guess the word got around and I was asked to audition for the Apollo and I sang there in between nights at the Easy Street. Well . . ." she let her words trail off.

Clayton picked up the story. "Salla's always shy about the next part. But I really don't know why. She and Terry Mc-Cord fell in love—they couldn't marry because he was already married and it was Salla's decision that he not get divorced—and, well, in time I was born. Salla stopped performing."

He looked at Salla and she made an impatient gesture. "You tell her the rest of it," she said.

Clayton said, "Terry always took good care of us, both of us. For some years I lived with Salla. And then Terry and Salla decided that I should go live and get an education in Europe, Ireland, for a time, so Terry made arrangements with his relatives and paid them for me to grow up there. Most of the rest of the story I told you when we had dinner was true. When Terry's wife, Rose, died, he moved Salla here and before he died he left me everything he owned."

Salla said softly, "That's it. That's the whole story."

Callie remembered now, the day they had videotaped the people at McCord's funeral, the woman whose face had been hidden behind a veil—the woman had been Salla.

They went into dinner then, four courses, served—Callie noted with hidden amusement—by an elderly English couple.

After dinner Salla excused herself and went upstairs and Callie and Clayton returned to the sitting room. Now with the two of them alone Callie for the first time became uneasy, remembering why she was there. She had sat down on the settee and Clayton, instead of returning to the piano stool, had joined her on the settee, which also made her uncomfortable. She said, "I think I'd better be leaving. I did have a lovely time and I do think your mother, Salla, is an enchanting person."

"Yes, of course," Clayton said, but he didn't get up. He

leaned across her and removed her handbag which was beside her and put in on a love seat that was out of her reach.

Callie made a move to stand but suddenly Clayton pushed her back on the settee, pinning her there with the weight of his body and gripping her by both wrists with one hand. Forced back, Callie struggled to get free. She felt his hand go up under her skirt and she struggled harder, clamping her legs together.

She felt his hand sliding up higher under her skirt and she began to thrash frantically around until she felt his hand yank free the .38 revolver she had secured in the waistband of her girdle, where she carried it sometimes instead of in her handbag. Clayton held up the revolver, aimed, from only a few inches away, straight at her head, and sat back, releasing her.

Clayton said, "I knew the gun had to be either in your pocketbook or your girdle, *Detective* Brinnin."

Callie collapsed against the back of the settee, no force needed to keep her immobile.

Clayton's face had hardened and his voice was harsh. "You tried to play me for a sucker, didn't you? All of you lousy cops. You underestimated me—you and a lot of other people, the lousy mob. You, the police, think you're the only ones who can get information? I've known about you, who you really were, almost since the first night you walked into the club."

Clayton was working himself into a fury and the more he talked the more terrified Callie became, realizing he'd never let her live after what he was spewing out in his blind anger.

"I beat them, do you understand? I beat the mob, beat them better than even Terry did. They were going to kill me! Do you understand that? I figured out a way to stop them, to get rid of them, and nobody'll ever be able to prove how I did it or that I did it. But then you, the cops, have to come after me. You and the D.A. and the whole damn police department."

Clayton kept the gun aimed at Callie's head. He went on talking. "Terry, my father, was always a hero to me. I admired the way he managed to get in on the action that's pretty much controlled by the mob. I wanted to be like him, to be in on the money and the power he had, and when he died and I got my chance I was ready and I took his place. And I'm going to stay where I am and nobody, not the mob, not the police, is going to get me."

He was silent, looking at her.

Callie knew it was meaningless to ask but she felt she had to say something about herself, that to remain silent would make it too easy for him. "What about me? What are you going to do about me?"

Some of Clayton's anger seemed to evaporate. "I'm afraid there's no choice. You're going to disappear from the face of the earth."

"What about Salla?" Callie asked. "What are you going to tell her about me, about what's happened to me?"

"She won't know anything about it. You'll be gone and in time I'll just tell her we've stopped seeing each other."

21

Midmorning the next day Charley Stenten was back in Lieutenant Frank Cavenaugh's office at the 16th Precinct. Cavenaugh, grinning, rocked back in his swivel chair. "I owe you a drink at that bar of yours, Dresner's, Charley. Thanks to you we can put the Krager-Shuba shooting deaths in the closed file. That punk Peter Holmer confessed that everything his girlfriend told you was true. Once he got the lawyer he'd hired and the lawyer read her statement, the lawyer told him he was finished. Holmer signed a confession that he was trying to extort money from Bettina Krager. He's hoping for a deal."

"Well, okay." Stenten smiled. "I thought he'd fold once he was confronted with Bonnie Seywood's statement to us."

"He admitted he didn't know a damn thing about the shooting that would involve Bettina Krager. He'd just pieced together some things Kenneth Shuba had told him before the shooting and decided to try to put the arm on Mrs. Krager. He admitted that he believed even if she wasn't involved she'd pay him off to keep him from telling us what he thought and getting her involved. The truth was he didn't know a single fact that could implicate her. When she wouldn't bite he panicked and was going to run, afraid that she would come to us with his extortion attempt."

Stenten said, "The boss'll be glad that at least this one is closed."

Cavenaugh reached for a pen and paper. "I'm going to write a final report for the file later. Check me out on my surmises based on what Bonnie Seywood and Holmer told us."

"Sure." Stenten nodded.

"As I see it," Cavenaugh said, "apparently Richard Krager suckered Kenneth Shuba step-by-step into a plot, probably with the promise that he'd provide the money for Shuba's porno films. At first, it was going to be a robbery Shuba would pull off and Krager would put in an inflated insurance claim. Right?"

"That's the way I read it," Stenten agreed.

"And then Krager upped the ante, according to what Holmer says Shuba told him, to do something bigger than a robbery. For which Krager would pay Shuba one hundred thousand dollars."

Stenten nodded.

Cavenaugh said, "Now, of course, we don't know what that something bigger was but do we agree we can surmise what it might have been?"

"With the gun Shuba had, with the fact that Krager had to have provided Shuba with a key to the apartment and with the information about the time the doorman would likely be lax on duty, I think we can safely surmise what Krager wanted Shuba to do."

"Say it, Charley."

"You say it, Frank."

Cavenaugh said, "Kill Krager's wife. That had to be it. And it would look like a bungled robbery."

"Yep. That would be my surmise," Stenten said. "All

along the plot Krager had in mind was for Shuba to kill Bettina Krager."

Cavenaugh was making notes as they talked. "Only something screwed up. Shuba shot and killed Krager by accident—Krager must have come out of the bedroom at the top of the stairs at the wrong time, Shuba thought it was Mrs. Krager and fired his gun—and then Mrs. Krager got her husband's gun and shot and killed Kenneth Shuba, thinking he really was a burglar."

"It all hangs together," Stenten said, "based upon all the circumstances we've put together."

Cavenaugh put down his pen. "Good! That's the way I'm going to write it up. Agreed?"

"Agreed."

"I have a surprise for you." Cavenaugh stood. "Mrs. Krager was in here just before you came. I sent for her to tell her the case was closed. I told her you were the one who cracked it. She wants to thank you in person. She's waiting in another office. I thought you and I should talk before you saw her."

"Hang on a minute, Frank. You didn't tell her you thought the whole thing was a plot on her husband's part to kill her, did you?"

"I couldn't tell her that," Cavenaugh said. "Actually, we don't have any hard proof of that. But I think she suspects it. I wanted her to know that we had nailed Holmer on the extortion plot."

Stenten was frowning. "Did she tell you why she never reported Holmer to the police?"

"She said honestly that she was afraid we might believe Holmer. And since she knew what he was saying was a lie and she wasn't going to pay him off, she decided to do nothing. I guess that's understandable. Come on, let's go."

As they walked to an office two doors away from Cavenaugh's office, Stenten said, "I hope it's not going to be too

155

much of a shock for her when she sees me and finds out who I really am, the guy she once had lunch with."

They walked into the office and Bettina smiled when Cavenaugh said, "Mrs. Krager, this is the man you wanted to thank for closing the case on your husband's death. This is Lieutenant Charley Stenten, of the district attorney's office."

Bettina took Stenten's hand and gave no indication that she recognized him. "Thank you so very much, Lieutenant. I'm glad the whole nightmare is finally coming to an end."

Stenten nodded. "I'm sure you are, Mrs. Krager. We are too."

Bettina said, "Thank you, too, Lieutenant Cavenaugh. I'll be going now."

"I'll go down with you," Stenten said. "I have to get back to my office." He gave a wave of his hand to Cavenaugh. "I'll be talking to you, Frank."

Stenten and Bettina went downstairs.

It wasn't until they were out of the building that Stenten said, "You didn't seem surprised at seeing me again, Mrs. Krager, and learning who I really am. I didn't mean to deceive you the day we had lunch. It just wasn't the time to tell you."

"That's all right." She tilted her head, an amused expression on her face. "I'd guessed by the day we had lunch who you were. That is, that you were a detective, part of the investigation of Richard's murder."

Stenten was puzzled. "How in the world could you have guessed who I was?"

"Because"—she was watching him, still with amusement—"I'd seen you before."

"Before? When?"

"The day what's his name, Holmer, first approached me in front of the Plaza Hotel—after he'd earlier phoned me and warned me I'd better meet him. I noticed you following me when I left my apartment and saw you watching in front of the Plaza."

"I'm amazed," Stenten said. "I thought I was better at surveillance than that!"

Bettina laughed. "Don't be too hard on yourself. I've had experience spotting people following me. For a while Richard had a team of private detectives keeping track of where I went, whom I saw. I got used to watching around me."

"Why would your husband have private detectives following you?"

"It's part of a long story. Look, it's after the noon hour. Are you free to have lunch? I'd like to treat you for the help you've been to me."

"It's not necessary for you to treat me," Stenten said. "But I would like to have lunch with you, yes. As a matter of fact I know a little French restaurant not far from here, Colette's the name. Would you care to try it?"

"Yes."

They walked four blocks to Colette's, a cozy restaurant seven steps down from street level in the West Forties. There were red-checkered cloths on the tables, and a waiter brought them hot fresh-baked bread and pâté with the bottle of Chablis they ordered.

"I like it here," Bettina said. "And I have to tell you something else, Charley Stenten, I like you too. I was hoping we'd see each other again. But I knew if we ever did, it wouldn't be until the investigation ended. And that's the way it worked out; here we are."

"Tell me something," Stenten asked, "the day we had lunch and you were pretty sure I was a detective, why didn't you tell me Peter Holmer was trying to extort money from you when I asked you about him? You say you liked me then and clearly you knew that I liked you, so why didn't you tell me about him?"

Bettina said slowly, "Yes, I did know you liked me; I could tell. But, after all, I suspected you were a detective and—well, now I'll tell you the same thing I told Lieutenant Cavenaugh—I was afraid you just might believe Holmer."

Stenten laughed. "No way. Sooner or later I'd have found a way to get the truth out of him." He was quiet for a moment, then said, "It's not really important but earlier when I asked you why your husband was having you followed, you said it was part of a long story. If you'd like to tell me more, I'd like to hear."

"I don't mind telling you," she said. "If you and I are going to get to know each other better, I want you to know."

She took a sip of wine. "Richard was a very mixed-up man. I didn't know that when I married him, of course. He considered himself to be shrewd but actually he was pretty stupid. I think the only reason he married me was to show me off. It was a terrible, terrible, terrible marriage. We were almost never together except when he wanted us to go out together in public so we could be seen and often photo-graphed. When I say we were almost never together other-wise, that includes—well, in bed. He just wasn't interested, ever." She stopped talking, blushing suddenly. "This must sound awful to you."

"No," Stenten said. "I know such things happen. I'm just sorry for you."

"Anyhow, he realized fairly soon that I was unhappy. Then he began to suspect I was going to leave him, divorce him. He was always asking me where I went, whom I saw, finally to the point of hiring private detectives to follow me. We were both miserable."

"If he knew it was such a miserable marriage, as you say, why would he want you to go on with it?"

"Two reasons," she said. "One, he was very vain, very conscious of his image. *Nobody* was going to divorce him. The second reason, and the reason he wouldn't think of divorcing me is that when we married there was no prenuptial agree-ment. In the event of a divorce he was afraid he'd wind up having to pay me a small fortune."

Stenten was turning his wineglass around and around in his hand. "I see."

Bettina said softly, "That's why he wanted me killed. Why he hired someone to kill me."

Stenten knew Cavenaugh hadn't told her the police had concluded her husband had hired Shuba to kill her.

Stenten asked, "You knew he wanted you dead before the night of the shootings?"

She looked at him wide-eyed and nodded.

"How did you know?"

"I—overheard things. I knew the night they planned to do it, and how. The key Richard gave to Shuba, the instructions of the time to enter the building, even—" she looked directly into Stenten's eyes—"even where Richard would hide the unlicensed gun, near the foot of the stairs, Shuba was to use. I told you Richard was stupid. He never stopped to consider that whatever he might do to check on me I might be equally capable of doing to check on him."

She sat back in her chair, her eyes on him, giving him time before he said whatever he was going to say next.

There it all was, finally, Stenten thought, and was not surprised. *She knew her husband had planned to have her killed. How? She was equally capable of checking on him—with private detectives—as he was on her, she said. She had—overheard things. It would have been simple for a private detective to put a tap on the phone, it was in her own house, and she was the only one who heard the tap. She overheard, as she put it, all the rest of it—even where her husband had put the unlicensed gun Shuba was to use.*

Stenten could conjecture the rest of it: *At the time Shuba entered the apartment, she had been waiting on the staircase with her husband's .38 revolver. She shot Shuba and killed him, went down the stairs, took the unlicensed .380 automatic her husband had hidden, and waited. When Richard Krager came rushing out of the bedroom at the top of the stairs, she had shot and killed him. She placed one gun beside Shuba at the bottom of the stairs, the other beside her husband at the top of the stairs. She had admitted firing a gun. She didn't have to worry about a paraffin test on her hands. She went to the phone and called the police. She had saved her own life.*

If it were all publicly known, Stenten concluded, *after long legal wrangling a strong case could be made that she was acting in self-defense. As it was, no one could ever prove what she had done, not even he, despite what she had told him, and an equally strong case could be made that there was about it a sense of justice prevailing.*

Stenten could live with that.

He said, "I do understand, Bettina."

"You do, don't you," she said, "all of it."

"Yes."

"And it doesn't make any difference—between you and me—for the future?"

"It doesn't make any difference," Stenten said.

What he didn't say was that he wasn't all that sure there would ever be a future for the two of them. Right now she was very vulnerable, and she did feel something for him, trusted him. Trusted him enough to tell him everything she'd told him, even if they both knew he could never prove what she'd told him. Right now, because she was vulnerable, he with his gun and badge represented power and protection to her. Every cop knew there were sometimes situations like this. But in time things changed and who knew whether they'd really have a future together.

Rebecca Cohen could hardly contain her indignation enough to speak.

"Can you believe it? Judge Morrison just released Lewis Bevvers when his one-million-dollar bail was posted! How could the judge do that? Let him out?"

Anne could sympathize with the distress of her assistant D.A. What she answered was, "A better question is who posted the bail money to release him?"

"I couldn't find that out, of course," Rebecca said. "All the record will show is that Bevvers's lawyer, Martin Groger, arranged the posting of the bail. Nothing I could say when I

was notified to attend the bail hearing in court dissuaded the judge."

Rebecca had interrupted a meeting between Anne and John Holland to give her the news about the release of Bevvers. Holland had arrived at Anne's office only a few minutes before Rebecca appeared and he and Anne had not had an opportunity to talk together alone, so Anne had asked him to remain.

Holland asked, "Were you able to arrange for surveillance on Bevvers after he left the courtroom?"

"That I did do," Rebecca said. "Detective Steve Alison, who's been on the case all along, went to court with me. He'd already arranged a surveillance team to follow Bevvers from then on, in the event that the judge released him. When Bevvers left the courthouse he was followed and Steve Alison assured me we'll be told where Bevvers is living."

"Good," Anne said. "I'll assign Charley Stenten to maintain surveillance on Bevvers. Cavenaugh informed me they've closed the file on the Krager case. I'll tell you about it later. So, Stenten's available to keep watch on Bevvers."

Holland added, "It'll be interesting to see where Bevvers goes now, to see what he does."

Anne said, "Rebecca, I want you to believe, once more, that you have done everything anybody could do to make sure that justice is done in this case."

Rebecca nodded. "All right, boss, if you say so I believe it."

Anne pointed a finger. "Furthermore, Lewis Bevvers is a long way from being finished with us."

Rebecca smiled, nodded again, and left the office after saying she was encouraged by the supporting words from Anne and Holland.

Alone again, Anne said, "I don't know how the Bevvers case is going to eventually end but right now, John, there's a more urgent matter we need to discuss."

Holland listened quietly as Anne told him of the conversation she had had with Arthur Hillyard the night before.

"This has to be the work of Russell Cody," Holland said when she finished talking. "But as far as having a tape of a conversation between you and me is concerned, I don't see how that's possible."

"Nor do I," Anne said. "But if it is Cody, why would he be doing it, tape or no tape?"

Holland spread his hands. "Beats me. Unless Cody is some kind of zealot and is trying to strike at you because he believes you didn't think enough of him and his charges when he first told you his suspicions about Grisham. In that case it would be my fault for having talked you into delaying any official action against Hank Grisham until I saw what I could find out. If you want me to make a statement to that effect to anyone anywhere, I'll do it."

"I know that, John. At the moment I don't see how that would help, since no one's officially accused me, or you, of anything."

Anne was interrupted by the intercom on her desk. Jenny Corso told her Lieutenant Frank Cavenaugh was in the outer office and had asked that Anne be informed he had to see her briefly on an urgent matter that couldn't be delayed.

"Tell Lieutenant Cavenaugh I'll see him now," Anne said, and then to Holland, "John, will you step outside for a minute, please? Frank Cavenaugh says it's urgent he sees me."

"Of course."

Holland left the office and Cavenaugh came in quickly, closing the door securely behind him. Cavenaugh didn't waste words. He took a manila envelope from under his coat and put it on the corner of Anne's desk.

"Ask me no questions. I heard about and managed to get a copy of what's inside the envelope. I thought you should

have it. Open the envelope after I've gone." Cavenaugh
turned and went out.

Anne opened the envelope and lifted out the small cassette tape. She leaned forward and said over the intercom,
"Send Lieutenant Holland back in, please, Jenny."

Anne had taken a tape recorder from her desk drawer
and was inserting the cassette when Holland came back into
the office. She didn't try to make any explanation. She turned
on the recorder and she and Holland listened.

*"John, a sergeant in Internal Affairs, a Russell Cody, was
waiting for me after work today. He said he had to talk to me about
a confidential matter. We talked alone in my car. He said Roy
Clayton was tipped off in advance of the raid on the warehouse in the
Bronx when we'd hoped to catch Clayton. He said Clayton's getting
inside information from the police department. Sergeant Cody says
that one of your men, one of the men on the Organized Crime Task
Force, is being paid off by Roy Clayton. He says the detective is Henry
Grisham . . ."*

*"No way is what Cody told you true. I know Hank Grisham . . .
He's had some personal problems . . . but there's no way he'd sell out
the department . . . What I'm asking is that we cover for Hank . . .
Is it a deal?"*

"Okay . . . It's a deal."

The tape ended. Anne turned off the recorder.

"Son of a bitch!" Holland exploded. "That tape's been
doctored. You and I never had the conversation that's on
that tape!"

Anne appeared stunned. "No, of course we didn't. But—
but—do you realize when we *did* have the conversation that's
been edited into what's on that tape? It was on the same
night, the very same night, of the late afternoon that Cody
first approached me and told me about Detective Grisham.
Which means—"

"Which means," Holland said, "Cody already knew
about you and me."

163

"But how could he have known?"

"I can only think the way it must have happened was that he was running an investigation on Hank Grisham—as we know he was. And because I was Grisham's superior Cody did a brief surveillance on me and picked up that you and I have a relationship."

"Okay," Anne said, "but how does that explain why he would have been eavesdropping on us the same night he first approached me about Grisham?"

"Because," Holland said, "clearly he was looking for some kind of conspiracy involving Grisham and me and maybe you. He may have gotten a court order or the bug may have been illegal, just as the tape has been doctored. He could have just been on a fishing expedition. If he hadn't picked up anything damaging from our conversation he would have destroyed the tape."

"But the tape can't be used in court."

Holland shrugged. "He may not care about that. It might be enough for him that with the tape he believes he can create serious trouble for you and me."

"Why would he want to do that?"

"That, my darling, is a good question. Maybe there's something more behind it. There may be someone who wants to strike at me, or you, and the investigation of Grisham provided the opportunity."

Anne asked, "So, what do I do now? What do we do?"

Holland shook his head. "Nothing. We have to wait it out and see what happens. Meantime, though, I'd like to take the tape to an electronics expert I know. I'm sure he'll be able to determine that somebody fooled around with it."

"Take it," Anne said.

Holland put the tape back into the envelope and jammed it into his coat pocket. "I'll let you know what I find out." Then he sat back in the chair. "There's another problem."

"What?"

"Yesterday afternoon Callie Brinnin told me she received a call from Roy Clayton. She was going out with him last night. This morning she didn't report for work. And nobody's heard from her."

"You think something's happened to her?"

"I don't know what to think," Holland said. "But I'm not taking any chances. According to the Police Intelligence Unit, Clayton lives in the house he also inherited from Terrence McCord on Staten Island. Before I came here I sent a couple of men to stake out the house. If Callie's cover was blown for some reason and he's holding her, chances are it would be there. In fact, there are a couple of things I want to do first, like getting this tape into the hands of the guy I know, and then I'm going to head over to Staten Island myself and join the stakeout at Clayton's house. Right now, trying to find out what happened to Callie takes priority."

"Absolutely," Anne agreed.

"I'll keep in touch with you," Holland said.

He kissed her and left.

22

Anne went into the office on Saturday, giving up her day for shopping. During the week a stack of paperwork had accumulated that needed her attention. Jenny had volunteered to come in so they could catch up on the dictation and typing. Anne could have asked one of the other secretaries to work the extra time but she preferred to have Jenny. "You're a dear to help me out today," she told her.

"It's called making Brownie points, boss."

Jenny had already divided the papers into two piles. One only required Anne's handwritten notes or signature, the other needed letters in answer. So for the next two hours Anne dictated and Jenny took the words down in shorthand, then went off to type the letters. Anne concentrated on going through the other pile of papers.

A few minutes before noon Anne's beeper signal went off. She knew that both John Holland and Charley Stenten were on stakeout and she supposed it was one or the other of them trying to reach her.

When she dialed back the number on the beeper's readout Charley Stenten answered and said, "I'm over here in Queens, watching the house where Lewis Bevvers is holed up. There's just been a development. A car pulled up in front of his house and three men, big guys, got out and went up to the door. I saw Bevvers come to the door and it looked like they pushed him inside."

"Did you call for backup, Charley?"

"That's the hell of it," Stenten said. "My car phone's gone dead. I'm in a phone booth and I only had change to make one call. I thought I'd better not take a chance of calling headquarters and not being able to get through to somebody. That's why I'm calling you."

Anne said, "Give me the address. I'll call for backup. And I'm coming over there myself. Be there as soon as I can."

She disconnected after Stenten gave her the location where he was and directions how to get there. Then she called headquarters and ordered the dispatcher there to get a backup unit to the address in Queens. She went out of her office, told Jenny there was an emergency she had to investigate, and said that Jenny could leave after she'd finished typing the letters.

"I'll sign them Monday." She gave Jenny a wave and left.

She'd driven her own car down to the office that morning and she got it out of the parking lot and headed up the FDR Drive to Forty-ninth Street, across to First Avenue and on to Fifty-seventh Street for half a block and turned onto the ramp heading to the Queensboro Bridge.

The address Stenten had given her was in Woodside, Queens, not far from the bridge. She had never been in Woodside before in her life, a place of narrow streets and rundown houses and buildings, but she had no trouble following the directions Stenten had given her. He had told her his car was parked near the corner in the block next to the one where the address he'd given her was located.

She noted the house as she drove past it and on to the

next block. Stenten was in his car there. She parked in the middle of the block and walked back to Stenten's car.

Stenten eased the car door open and she got inside. He was looking back over his shoulder at the house in the next block, which was only a few doors away from the corner. He said, "No backup yet. The guys are still inside with Bevvers. Nothing else has happened. So what do we do now?"

"We can't go barging in there without a search warrant. And we have no probable cause for getting a warrant, even if there was time. For all we know, the four of them inside could be playing bridge—"

"Hey! Hey!" Stenten interrupted her. "They're coming out of the house!"

Anne turned to watch.

One man came out first, followed by two others more or less half dragging Lewis Bevvers. The men shoved Bevvers into the backseat of the car, a four-door Chrysler LeBaron sedan, parked in front of the house.

Stenten started the engine of his car as the three men climbed into the Chrysler, two of them in the backseat with Bevvers, the other man driving. As the car pulled away, Stenten made a U-turn to follow, at a distance.

Anne said, "Well, I guess they weren't there to play bridge."

As the Chrysler up ahead led them back toward the Queensboro Bridge, Anne and Stenten could hear the sound of distant sirens behind them. "The cavalry to the rescue," Stenten said dryly. "Too little, too late. Headquarters is going to want to know why the district attorney ordered them out on a wild-goose chase."

"Yeah, yeah." Anne said.

They kept the Chrysler LeBaron in sight back over the Queensboro Bridge and down the FDR Drive to lower Manhattan and then west from the drive into Little Italy near the point where Little Italy intersected with Chinatown. It finally came to a stop on a side street alongside a dry cleaning shop at the corner. The street the dry cleaning shop faced on had only a few buildings in the block, a couple of tenements, a small grocery store, and next to the dry cleaning shop, a building with a darkened plate glass window that had on it in gold lettering Furelli Funeral Home.

Stenten let his car idle a half a block away as he and Anne watched the three men emerge from the Chrysler, dragging Lewis Bevvers between them, and disappear into a side door of the dry cleaning shop. Once the men were out of sight he drove slowly forward past the dry cleaning shop and turned into an alley behind the shop when he saw the shop had no windows or doors looking out into the alley. He stopped the car there. From that spot they'd be able to see the other car if it drove past the alley.

"Now, we really better get some backup here," Anne said.

"Yeah." Stenten looked around. "Why don't you wait here, keep an eye on things. I'll go try to find a phone booth. Uh—you have any change?"

"I think so." Anne lifted her handbag, reached inside, and handed Stenten several quarters, nickels, and dimes.

Stenten slid out of the car and disappeared down the alley.

Anne put her handbag back on the floor of the car and sat watching the street at the end of the alleyway. There was a stillness in the heat of early afternoon. She had to keep brushing away the flies that buzzed in through the open car windows.

She was taken by surprise when the two men appeared from the rear of the car, one on either side, and yanked open both the car's front doors. The man nearest her grabbed her arm and pulled her out of the car. The other man slid across the front seat and out behind her, clamping a hand around the back of her neck. They propelled her to the top of the alley, around the corner, and into the same side door of the dry cleaning shop through which Lewis Bevvers had disappeared.

Everything had happened with such unexpected swiftness that she had only a disjointed impression of what the men looked like: Both were big, tall as well as muscular, but beyond that she had no clear image of them. This was the first time in her life that she had been physically manhandled. She understood now as she had never understood before why it was so difficult for witnesses, victims, to make positive identifications in cases where physical violence was involved.

By then it was too late for her to get a clearer look at either of the men who had attacked her. Once inside the shop, one of the men slapped a blindfold of some kind of cloth over her eyes and the other man plastered a wide strip of adhesive tape over her mouth. Unable to see and silenced, she stood helpless as she felt her arms yanked behind her back and her wrists tied together. Then, stumbling awkwardly, she was led by one of the men while the other prodded her forward. She heard a door open and chill air along with a foul odor enveloped her. She was led and prodded several more steps before she was brought to a stop and forced down into a wooden chair. She felt her whole body trembling, trembling, and she couldn't will the trembling to stop.

John Holland sat in the unmarked police Ford Fairlane, a pair of binoculars at his eyes, watching Roy Clayton's house in Staten Island. The car was parked off the side of the road a distance from the house. Holland had been there since dawn and all he had been able to observe was the white-walled enclosure around the house, the wrought iron gate, and the two men who from time to time came out of the gatehouse next to the entrance to the driveway.

The house had been under police surveillance since the

day before by a shift of detectives—Holland himself had been there part of the previous day and night—and no one had been seen entering or leaving the place. It was now early afternoon.

A second unmarked car waited a mile up the road. Myler and Martino of Holland's Organized Crime Task Force were in that car. The men in the two cars communicated back and forth over the police radio. Holland spotted a car coming along the road and he switched on the radio. "Car approaching!" he reported. "Hang on."

"Roger!" Martino answered.

Holland slid down in his seat as the car came nearer, passed by Clayton's house, and was soon out of sight.

"False alarm," Holland said over the radio. He sat up in the seat again and focused the binoculars on Clayton's house.

Time passed.

Holland slid down in the seat again so he wouldn't be seen as a man and a woman on bicycles pedaled past and on around a bend in the road.

More time passed.

A jetliner appeared high in the sky to the east and streaked eastward out over the Atlantic Ocean.

Holland felt a cramp in his right leg from having sat still for so long. He was debating whether he could risk stepping out of the car to stretch his legs when he saw the two men at Clayton's gatehouse come out again and swing open the wrought iron gate. "This may be something!" he said quickly into the radio as a black Lincoln sedan rolled out through the gate and turned on the road headed toward Holland.

Tense, Holland kept the binoculars trained on the windows of the Lincoln, desperately trying to get a look at who was inside the car, delaying ducking down out of sight for as long as he dared. In the last moments he knew he had before the Lincoln got close enough so he would be seen, he had one quick glimpse of the passengers in the other car, the driver whom he didn't recognize and Clayton in the front seat and—

Holland almost wanted to shout out—Callie in the backseat, a man on either side of her.

Holland dropped to the floor of his car, out of sight, taking the radio with him, saying, his voice urgent, "This is it! A black Lincoln sedan coming your way! Callie's in it, along with Clayton and three other men! Get out ahead of it, try to keep it in sight in your rearview mirror! I'll be tailing it from behind! Maintain constant radio contact! Go!"

"Read you loud and clear," Myler answered. "We're moving out now."

Holland had already started up his car, the wheels spraying roadside gravel behind as he swung the car onto the pavement and headed after the Lincoln, coming in sight of the black sedan a mile ahead. He slowed his speed and dropped back a distance when he had the Lincoln in view at the same time that Myler's voice came over the radio. "The Lincoln's in sight well behind us. We'll try to maintain the same distance ahead of him."

"I have him in view too," Holland said. "Let's see where we're going."

Holland kept pace with the Lincoln at the same approximate distance as they turned onto the expressway and into a steady stream of traffic moving eastward.

Holland used the radio. "Looks like he's heading for the Verrazano Bridge."

"We still have him in sight behind us," Myler answered. "We figure the Verrazano too."

A few minutes later Myler added, "It's the Verrazano. We're on it and he's not too far behind us."

Holland, cutting in and out around the other cars crossing the bridge, managed to keep the black Lincoln always in sight on the trip through Brooklyn and up into lower Manhattan.

Myler was on the radio again. "He's still heading westward across town and getting closer behind us."

"If he gets too close, let him pass," Holland answered.

"Follow him from behind. I have him in the clear."

"He's just passed us," Myler said a minute later.

"Drop back! Drop back!" Holland ordered. "Drop behind me. It looks like our destination's Little Italy. Call the dispatcher to send in some other units."

"Roger."

Holland watched as he passed the car containing Myler and Marino and saw in his rearview mirror that they were now right behind him. The black Lincoln had turned into a side street, still in Little Italy but near to Chinatown.

Myler's voice came back over the radio. "Lieutenant, the dispatcher advises that Lieutenant Stenten of the D.A.'s office has already called in requesting backup units and the location he gave was this same street. The units are en route."

"Roger," Holland said, and wondered what the hell was going on. Why would Charley Stenten be somewhere around and calling for backup?

Up ahead the Lincoln had pulled over to the curb and parked.

Holland used the radio to order Myler and Martino to stay back while he drove on past the car up ahead in time to see Clayton, holding tight to Callie's arm, and the other three men enter a building near the corner. The building had the words Furelli Funeral Home lettered in gold on the dark plate glass window.

Holland drove on down the street, puzzled; the name of the funeral home was somehow familiar to him but he couldn't think why.

Roy Clayton, pushing Callie ahead of him, went in through the door of the Furelli Funeral Home without glancing back at the street as John Holland drove by. Neither did any of the other three men notice the car.

The door had been opened by Alfredo Furelli, a tall, thin man with sparse black hair, dark eyes, a black mustache that curved under his nose from one corner of his mouth to the other corner. Furelli raised a shaking hand and touched Clayton on the chest. "Please hurry," he implored. "Too much happening. Hurry, Hurry!"

Furelli closed the door and went ahead of Clayton down a hallway; the other three men, with Callie between them, followed.

Toward the rear of the building Furelli led the group through a second door into a large room with whitewashed walls and a tile floor, the room running the width of the building and lighted by glaring fluorescent tubes set in the ceiling. At one side of the room was a huge stainless steel sink the size of a bathtub. Above the sink were stainless steel shelves filled with bottles of chemicals. In front of the sink was the nude body of a young white female lying spread-eagled on a long metal table, a white rubber sheet covering the lower half of her body, a bare foot hanging out on either side of the sheet.

On the opposite side of the room was a row of a dozen large caskets lined up side by side, some of them closed, others with their satin-lined tops up. The air in the room was heavy with the sickening smell of formaldehyde.

Anne Gilman, blindfolded, her mouth covered with adhesive tape, her arms tied behind her, sat unmoving in a chair under one of the two windows in the back wall of the room.

Lewis Bevvers, also with his mouth covered by adhesive tape and his arms tied behind him, was in another chair near the back wall of the room.

Callie had felt her legs go weak under her when she'd first entered the room, struck by the overall bizarreness of the scene before her. As her vision focused more specifically she recognized Anne and almost cried out.

At that same moment Roy Clayton had pointed toward Anne and asked, "Who's she? Where did she come from?"

One of the men who had been in the room when Clayton and the others came in said, "We don't know who she is. Right after we got here with Bevvers I noticed through the window that a car had pulled into the back alley. She was in the car with a guy. I watched them. The guy got out and went away down the alley. She stayed in the car like she was watching. Me and the others decided maybe she and the guy were sent by one of the gangs to follow us here, maybe after they followed us here from where we picked up Bevvers. And the guy left the car to call somebody and set us up for a hit. We grabbed her and brought her in here. We came in through the dry cleaning shop. Nobody saw us. We blindfolded her in the shop so she wouldn't know we were bringing her in here and have her go crazy with fear and give us a hard time."

When Clayton waved a hand of dismissal in the air and said, "Whatever the hell it was, we'll deal with her later," Callie realized Clayton hadn't recognized Anne and didn't know who she was. Callie was glad she had kept quiet.

Furelli approached Clayton, whining, "What are we going to do now, Roy? If one of the gangs is going to hit this place—"

Clayton shoved Furelli away. "Just shut up, Alfredo."

One of the men who had been watching the alley from the window, called out, "Something fishy's going on, boss! There are guys coming into the alley from both ends!"

Clayton crossed to the window quickly and looked out. He saw eight or nine men, guns in their hands, moving into the alley. He thought for a split second that maybe they were going to be hit by one of the gangs. And then he saw a face he recognized: the cop, the lieutenant, who had come to warn him that night at the Easy Street Club that he was the target of a contract hit. Clayton moved back from the window and snapped his fingers. "It's not a hit! It's the cops! I don't know how they got here but they're going to be coming in! We have to move fast!"

"The cops!" Furelli wailed. "What are we going to do?"

"Move fast," Clayton said. He pointed to Callie. "Tape her mouth and tie her up." He pointed to Anne and Bevvers. "Then bury all three of them"—he turned and pointed to the caskets—"and I mean bury them deep! Then let the cops come in, we stay cool, they don't find anything, anybody, they go away. I'll handle them. Just stay cool. Hurry," he added as they heard pounding at the street door.

Anne, still blindfolded and tied in the chair, had heard everything that had been said but she couldn't make much sense out of what was going on in the room around her. She couldn't figure out who was doing most of the talking and she couldn't figure out who the third person in the room was who was to be gagged and tied up or why. She had heard whoever was doing most of the talking mention that there were cops outside which meant that Charley Stenten had made his call and they were about to break into the place. But how did the men in the room think nothing would happen once she and Bevvers were found?

Before she could think any further, she felt herself being lifted and carried across the room. She still couldn't understand what was happening as she was lowered into some kind of small enclosure, down, down, resting on her back, and aware that a top or lid was closing above her. Now she could hear nothing.

The space was small and cramped; she could feel that. Her body was touching the top and the bottom of the enclosure and both sides of it, and she had trouble breathing in the closed-in space. She fought down her incipient feeling of claustrophobia and tried to reason out what was happening and exactly where she was being confined. She thought back to the two men who had forced her out of the car in the alley and into the side door of the dry cleaning shop. She'd been inside before she'd been blindfolded. But then the men had walked her through a door and into some place where suddenly the air was chill and there was an overwhelming foul odor.

Her thoughts went connectively to what she had observed and forgotten: The dry cleaning shop was directly next to a funeral home! She had been brought into the funeral home and now, now, it finally penetrated her consciousness—oh Dear God, she was lying in a closed coffin! She fought to contain her terror and suppress claustrophobia, remembering that she had heard the police were there, Stenten had brought them, and surely, surely, surely, they wouldn't overlook such a likely place where she might have been hidden away. They'd open the lid to the coffin and there she'd be! She tried to hold on to that hope even as she struggled to fight down the waves of panic that swept through her.

Holland and Stenten stood at the entrance to the alley where Stenten's car was. The police who had responded to Stenten's urgent call for backup were all around them, in the front and back of the dry cleaning shop and the front and back of the funeral home next to the shop.

As soon as Holland had seen Clayton and the three men take Callie into the funeral home, he had parked his car up ahead. He then walked back to the corner where Myler and Martino joined him. Stenten, who had been keeping out of sight, appeared and he and Holland exchanged information about what had brought them separately to the same place. And they had waited then until the backup units arrived, nine squad cars, and two unmarked cars, twenty-two men in all. The funeral home and the dry cleaning shop were surrounded, the men waiting for Holland's command to move in.

Holland repeated a question he'd asked Stenten once before. "You're sure the men you saw took Anne in the side door of the dry cleaning shop?"

"I'm certain," Stenten answered again. "Anne and I had already seen them take Bevvers in through the same door. I had gone to find a phone booth and call the dispatcher for help. I was coming back through the alley when I saw the two men force Anne out of the car and into the shop. I was unarmed, I knew backup was on the way, so I took a position on the corner where I could observe the front and side of the shop. Nobody else went in or out."

Holland asked, "And you also had the front door of the funeral home in view?"

"All the time. The guys you know about entered but nobody left there, from the moment Anne was taken."

Holland nodded. "All right, you and I are going into the shop." He passed the word to Myler. "Tell the men waiting in front to go into the funeral home now!" To Stenten, he added, "Come on."

Holland and Stenten, followed by two detectives, crashed in through the door to the dry cleaning shop. The shop was small, with suits and dresses in plastic bags hanging on rods, no one there. They opened doors to two small cubicles, also empty.

There was a third door directly opposite the side entrance to the shop. Holland tried the door and when it wouldn't yield, the four men broke it open and saw the large room on the other side with whitewashed walls, a room suddenly filled with men, detectives, uniformed policemen who had come in from the front of the funeral home, seven other men and Roy Clayton.

"You, all of you, up against the wall!" Holland ordered. As several of the detectives converged on Clayton and the seven other men, Holland added, "Face the wall, hands against the wall."

The detectives quickly searched the men for weapons, recovering five revolvers.

Clayton turned his head and said, "What is all this? My friends and I came to visit my old friend, Alfredo, Alfredo Furelli"—he pointed to Furelli who was up against the wall—"and you come barging in here."

Holland remembered then why the name of the funeral home, Furelli, had seemed familiar to him; that day in the cemetery when he and his unit had videotaped Terrence

McCord's burial, the name Furelli Funeral Home had been embossed on a brass plate on the side of the hearse.

Clayton said, "I don't know what legal right you have for searching us. These guns you recovered from my friends, they're all licensed. And where's your search warrant for coming in here in the first place?"

Holland stepped in close to Clayton, "We don't need a search warrant. We have probable cause to support this action. In fact, three probable causes: the abductions of three individuals who were brought here by you; Lewis Bevvers, Callie Brinnin, and District Attorney Anne Gilman." Holland saw the sudden confused look on Clayton's face at the mention of Anne Gilman's name.

"We know they're here," Holland said, his voice hard. "You were seen bringing them here. And the place has been watched ever since. They're still here. Now, where are they?"

Clayton made a gesture with his hand. "I'm sure Alfredo, Mr. Furelli, would say feel free to search the premises. Am I right, Alfredo?"

Holland could see that Furelli looked terrified even as he nodded his head.

Stenten and several of the detectives had left the room while Clayton and the others were being patted down for weapons. Stenten returned and reported to Holland, "We've searched the whole place. There's no sign of them."

"Yeah," Holland said. "Well, there's another place we haven't looked."

He pointed to the twelve large caskets lined up in a row on the opposite side of the room, all with their lids closed. "Let's see what we find in them."

Holland, followed by Stenten, with Myler and a couple of other detectives joining them, moved to the caskets, Holland lifting the lid of the first one. The satin-lined interior was empty.

Holland moved on to the second casket. It was empty. So

was the third casket. The fourth, the fifth, the sixth, the seventh, the eighth, the ninth, the tenth, the eleventh, the twelfth—the last one—also empty.

The twelve caskets, lids up, were all empty.

Anne's whole body ached from lying, unable to move, in the boxlike prison where she was confined. It was getting harder to breathe and she tried to control the spasms of rapid heartbeats that came and went every time she was on the edge of total panic. The rapid heartbeats, the onset of moments of sheer panic, increased her need for more oxygen, using up what she knew was the limited amount of air in the tiny space around her. Now her great additional fear was that she would black out.

Muffled as the sounds from outside that came through to her were, they kept her aware of movement beyond the place where she was a prisoner. She was sure she heard voices, the words indistinguishable, near her, then somewhere above her. Was someone about to open the lid of what she was sure was her coffin? She had that momentary hope and then it was gone as the voices, the movement, receded, and there was only silence again.

Her breathing had become a ragged gasp.

Holland turned away from the last casket he'd opened and found empty. He was filled with bitter frustration. He'd been so sure he'd figured out where Anne and Callie and Bevvers had been hidden away.

"Now, are you satisfied?" Clayton called out from across the room. "I told you there was no one else here."

Holland looked at Clayton and wanted to smash the smirk off Clayton's face. He started to charge across the room toward Clayton but Stenten grabbed him by the arm, restraining him, saying softly, "Easy, easy, John, we'll take care of him later. I know how you feel. But right now we've got to think with a clear head. We *know* Anne and Callie have to be here somewhere. And Bevvers. We just have to figure out some way to find them."

"You're right," Holland said, calming down. He looked around the room. "They have to be inside this building." He started to pace. "If there was just some way—"

He stopped pacing in midstride. "I just thought of something!" he said, his voice exultant. "I want a man in every room of this place! I want you to listen and listen closely. Let me know if you hear anything."

After the detectives had fanned out through the funeral home, Holland strode quickly to the telephone and dialed. He listened briefly, then put down the receiver. "Now, I want absolute silence," he said.

He wandered around the room, hoping to hear a shout from one of the detectives in the other part of the building, and listening, himself, for the sound he wanted desperately to hear. He was pacing up and down again and his steps had taken him to the far side of the room, near the row of open caskets.

He had turned and was about to walk back when he heard, faintly, the sound he'd been hoping to hear. He shouted, "Here! Here!" hurrying along the row of caskets, the faint sound growing louder as he reached one of the open caskets in the middle of the row.

Stenten was there beside him as Holland leaned into the casket, shouting, "It's coming from here! Underneath the bottom of the inside!"

Holland and Stenten were clawing at the satin-lined bottom of the casket, ripping up the fabric and prying at the wooden boards under the fabric, the sound of Anne's beeper signal growing louder as they ripped up the boards, flinging them onto the floor.

Both men shouted at the sight of Anne, her beeper signal insistently sounding over and over from the pocket of her jacket. Holland was so glad he'd remembered she always carried her beeper with her wherever she went. They lifted her out tenderly, Holland fearfully feeling for a pulse in her throat, shouting, "She's alive! She's alive!"

With Holland and Stenten holding her between them, Holland gently pried away the tape from her mouth while Stenten removed the blindfold. Holland lowered his head to hers, until he felt her breath come finally against his face, the merest wisp of her breath, but soon it came stronger and stronger. Holland, watching her face, was holding his own breath until suddenly her eyes blinked open. She looked at him, dazed, blinked her eyes, her vision cleared, and she smiled weakly.

Holland looked up and yelled, "Quick! Rip open the other caskets! Callie must be in one of them!"

Stenten passed Anne over to Holland, who carried her across the room, yelling at Furelli, "I need some brandy! Do you have any brandy?"

"I get! I get!" Furelli answered eagerly, hurrying out of the room with Myler following him.

Holland sat, holding Anne in his lap, untying her bound wrists, glancing up to watch Stenten and some of the other detectives ripping up the bottoms of the remaining caskets.

There was a shout from Stenten as he lifted Callie out of another casket. She was still conscious and Stenten removed the tape from her mouth and untied her wrists. With Stenten's support she was able to walk slowly over to Holland and Anne.

Myler had returned with Furelli and a bottle of brandy. Holland fed Anne small sips of the brandy until she raised a hand and whispered, "It's all right, I'm okay."

Callie leaned forward and put a hand on Anne's cheek and Anne smiled at her as Holland kissed Callie gently and said, "Welcome back, both of you."

Stenten had returned to the search through the caskets. At the next to the last one, when the wooden boards at the bottom were pried away, Stenten took a step back and called out, "John, you're going to love this one! Guess who we've found? None other than the missing Slick Nick Dolayga, late of the Boglio crime family, shot and snatched from Salvatora's Café. Slick Nick's all embalmed, lying here under the bottom of the interior of the coffin, ready for burial."

Anne, who was sitting up and had heard Stenten's words, looked at Holland and said, "Well, we've finally found what we've been looking for, haven't we? Now, all we need is a court order *fast* to confiscate all the records of this place. Right now!"

All at once Holland, too, understood. He said, "I'll send Martino."

Stenten and several of the detectives were ripping up the interior of the one remaining casket. When the bottom boards were pulled out, Stenten leaned into the casket and slowly straightened up. Then he said, "I don't know that I'm particularly sorry to announce that Lewis Bevvers's luck has run out. He's stone-cold dead. Suffocated, I guess."

Holland pointed at Clayton and Alfredo Furelli. "Get them and the rest of their 'friends' out of here. We're going to book them on charges of kidnapping and a string of murder charges. I expect the consecutive sentences for some of them won't run for more than a thousand years."

As Holland scooped Anne up into his arms, she said, mockingly protesting, "Lieutenant, I want you to know I can walk under my own power."

"That may well be," Holland said, kissing her and not caring who might see him or hear him, "but from here on I'm not letting you out of my arms for very long at a time."

23

On Monday morning, near noon, when the police helicopter lifted off from Floyd Bennett Field in Brooklyn, Anne and Holland were aboard with the pilot and copilot. The helicopter rose straight out over the East River, Manhattan to the west, Brooklyn and Queens to the east. Below, a tanker, several police launches, and eight or ten private boats plowed through the water, heading up and down the river. Six other helicopters were in sight fanning out over one side of the river or the other.

Sam Berrington, who was piloting the helicopter Anne and Holland were on, said, "I guess the media people are all heading to see the same sights we want to see. Let's take a look in Queens first."

He banked to the east and dropped lower as the chopper came into view of the Centralia Cemetery in Queens, near the Nassau County line. When they were directly over the cemetery, Berrington slowed speed and circled the area.

Anne held a pair of binoculars to her eyes, which focused on the scene below. The cemetery was cluttered with an array of vehicles, Police Emergency Service trucks, a van from the medical examiner's office, squad cars, two ambulances. A cluster of people stood around one grave site watching as cemetery workers finished digging up the earth and lifting out a dirt-encrusted coffin. Anne could see the TV newsmen with their cameras filming the action. In the air a couple of other helicopters carrying TV crews were filming footage of the activity on the ground.

As the helicopter Anne was aboard continued to circle, she could see three other places in the cemetery where the same scene—coffins being dug up—was taking place, with vehicles, people, TV crews, gathered around the various open graves.

"A hell of a nightmarish sight," Holland said, viewing the activity below.

"It should make quite a picture on the six o'clock news," Berrington remarked. "Now, let's check out your other locations."

From Queens the helicopter flew to Brooklyn, observed a replay at the Corinthian Cemetery there of the scene they'd observed in Queens, flew on to Staten Island, and then swept over to New Jersey and in the cemeteries in each place below them were cars, trucks, vans, and people clustered around the dug-up burial places.

As the helicopter made its circular journey, constant reports were coming in over the police radio. As Anne listened she now knew she had been right about what she had suspected on Saturday in the Furelli Funeral Home.

On Saturday, after she had obtained a court order to confiscate Furelli's records, she had checked the dates and locations of the funeral home's legitimate burials over the past months and had compared those burials with the dates after which the various mob figures had disappeared.

Secretly, early on Sunday, after obtaining another court order to exhume the body of the most recent legitimate Furelli burial, she, Holland, and a Police Emergency Service crew had gone to the Stonedge Cemetery in the Bronx. There the crew, with the help of some of the cemetery workers, had opened the grave of a Maria Lucerne. They had retrieved the casket, opened it, and removed the embalmed body of Maria Lucerne. Then they had pried up the bottom of the casket—and were lucky. Lying in the cramped compartment beneath was a second body, the body of Dino Capri who had disappeared after he was snatched off the street in front of his house in Hoboken. Anne knew that with the discovery of Capri's body they had cracked the case against Roy Clayton.

As she suspected, once Alfredo Furelli was confronted with the fact that they had recovered Capri's body in one of his coffins, Furelli would almost surely supply corroborating evidence.

Late Sunday afternoon, Alfredo Furelli, who was being held in the Metropolitan Correctional Center, was brought into police headquarters and interrogated. Anne was present while John Holland conducted the interrogation, along with Myler, Martino, and Callie Brinnin. Police Commissioner Clarkson also attended. Holland showed Furelli photos the police had taken earlier at the cemetery in the Bronx. The photos showed Maria Lucerne's body being removed from the coffin and Capri's body lying in the underneath compartment.

Alfredo Furelli talked, he talked eagerly, the words pouring out of him, along with the sweat of fear streaming down his face, soaking his shirt and jacket. Yes, all the bodies of the members of the mob gangs killed by Clayton and his gang had been brought to the funeral home and concealed under the bodies of whose who were to receive legitimate burials. Clayton had forced Furelli to do what he did.

How?

Blackmail.

Almost in a dreamlike state Furelli recounted how it all had come about, starting the story at the beginning. His wife had a first cousin, a man, who had come to her, pleading, with a problem. The cousin had said he had been living with a woman who had had an accident in their apartment. The woman had fallen, hit her head, and died. The cousin had said the police wouldn't believe it was an accident if he told them. The police would believe the cousin had killed the woman. The cousin had assured Furelli's wife that the woman wouldn't be missed if there was just some way she could disappear forever.

The cousin had come to ask for help because he knew Alfredo ran a funeral home and maybe there was some way Alfredo could help him dispose of the body. Maybe, the cousin had suggested, the body could be buried along with another body. Nobody would ever know. The wife kept after Furelli to help her cousin. After all, the woman had died accidentally.

Furelli's wife kept nagging him. Finally Furelli had agreed to dispose of the body. But the woman's body couldn't just be buried along with someone else. The coffin might be opened. Furelli had worked out a different solution. He talked to the company that constructed the coffins he used. He suggested they build a separate compartment at the bottom of a coffin for him. He told the casket company the compartment would keep water from the ground from leaking into the bottom of the coffin.

The company built him the coffin he wanted. The body of the woman who had died in the accident, which had been embalmed and kept at the funeral home, went into the grave in the bottom of somebody else's coffin. As the wife's cousin had said, nobody knew.

But then the cousin was arrested and charged as the murderer of another woman, possibly several other women. Furelli's wife's cousin was Lewis Bevvers.

Alfredo Furelli was frantic with worry, afraid that Bevvers, the cousin, actually had murdered the woman he had secretly buried. He had to talk to somebody about his terrible fear. He had known Terrence McCord all his life, they had been childhood friends, and he knew that McCord did things that weren't—legitimate.

So Furelli went to McCord and told him the whole story, asking McCord what he should do. McCord told Furelli not to worry, that if Bevvers tried to involve Furelli in his crimes, he, McCord, knew ways to take care of Bevvers.

What McCord didn't tell Furelli, and Furelli didn't know until after McCord was dead, was that McCord had told Roy Clayton everything Furelli had confided in him.

Later, Clayton had come to Furelli, telling him what he knew, telling Furelli he would tell the police unless Furelli agreed to dispose of in similar fashion certain bodies Clayton would bring to him. Worse, Furelli added, he was certain that Clayton would kill him if he didn't agree to this. So, he had ordered additional coffins with the added compartments and had done what Clayton ordered him to do. Sometimes the victims were brought in through the side door of the dry cleaning shop—which was only a front—so people who might have noticed wouldn't pay any attention.

Furelli was near collapse at this point in his story but Holland had an additional question: After Bevvers had been freed on bail, why did Clayton have Bevvers brought to the funeral home?

Furelli knew that answer as well. Clayton had put up the bail money, through the lawyer, to get Bevvers out of jail. Clayton, in establishing himself as head of McCord's operation and not wanting any loose ends around that might foul things up, wanted Bevvers out so he could kill him. He wasn't going to chance Bevvers ever finding out, or figuring out, that the bodies of the men he was killing were being disposed of in the same way as the woman Bevvers had had secretly buried—through Furelli's funeral home. He wasn't going to chance the possibility that Bevvers could use that information in a deal with the police.

Furelli was so eager to help Anne and Holland in the

investigation that as he neared the end of the interrogation he went over the records Anne had confiscated and tried to pinpoint the graves where they would find the bodies of Clayton's gangland victims.

With Clayton in custody, some of the developing story of Anne's investigation was reported on the news Sunday night. Because of this, early on Monday morning Sergeant Russell Cody of Internal Affairs turned himself in to Holland, hoping to make a deal before Clayton exposed him.

Cody, tugging at his shirt collar, had made a videotaped confession:

"I was running a check on Detective Henry Grisham when I was approached by Roy Clayton and offered a bribe if I would undertake certain services for him. Clayton came across me because he had got this girl, Aggie Martin was her name, to make up to Grisham, see what she could get out of him, because he knew Grisham was part of the Organized Crime Task Force that was on his tail. When Clayton found out I knew that you and D.A. Gilman were having a thing, which might not be viewed favorably if it was known, he worked out a plan to frame both of you. If you wonder how I knew about the two of you it was because of tailing Grisham, seeing you with Grisham, and then tailing you. Anyhow, Clayton planned this whole thing where it would look like it was Grisham working for him, not me, and that when I told this to D.A. Gilman, it would look like the two of you were trying to cover it up. Especially after Grisham was out of the way. Grisham didn't commit suicide. Clayton had him killed. Far as I know he had the girl, Aggie, killed too. Or at least she disappeared. But I want it clear I had nothing to do with any killings. And, yeah, I made the fake bugs of you and the D.A., too. Clayton said we had to have the tape if we were going to frame the two of you."

Cody's confession ended there.

*   *   *

Now, as the police helicopter completed its tour over the various cemeteries and headed back to Floyd Bennett Field, Anne made a last check of the list she was keeping as reports came over the police radio.

"Joey Rocco," Anne said, repeating the name of the last body reported as being recovered and identified. "That's all of them." She handed the list to Holland. "We did it, John. It's really all over."

"Hey, District Attorney Gilman," Berrington said, "did you just hear that latest report on the radio?"

Anne shook her head. "No. What?"

"They said there's a big crowd waiting at Floyd Bennett Field to greet you and Lieutenant Holland. TV people, reporters, the police commissioner, even somebody from the governor's office. The two of you are going to be big celebrities."

"Uh huh," Anne said, smiling, but not sure she liked what was coming.

Holland, who knew her well enough to sense what she was feeling, said quickly, "Just remember what we've often said about other people, other events, at times like this: It's a moment of exposure, and then life moves on."

She had to laugh. She kissed him and said, "That sounds like something my father would have said."